# THE ICE DUCHESS
PREQUEL TO THE DUCHESS SOCIETY SERIES

TRACY SUMNER

Copyright © 2020 by Tracy Sumner

The Ice Duchess was previously published in the anthology „A Scandalous Christmas" (2020).

All rights reserved.

Cover Design by Victoria Cooper

Edited by Casey Harris-Parks

Paperback ISBN: 979-8521259540

No part of this book may be reproduced in any form or by any electronic or mechanical means, including information storage and retrieval systems, without written permission from the author, except for the use of brief quotations in a book review.

ALSO BY TRACY SUMNER

**The Duchess Society Series**
The Ice Duchess *(Prequel)*
The Brazen Bluestocking *(coming September 2021)*
The Scandalous Vixen *(coming 2021)*
The Wicked Wallflower *(coming 2022)*

**League of Lords Series**
The Lady is Trouble
The Rake is Taken
The Duke is Wicked
The Hellion is Tamed

**Garrett Brothers Series**
Tides of Love
Tides of Passion
Tides of Desire: A Christmas Romance

**Southern Heat Series**
To Seduce a Rogue
To Desire a Scoundrel: A Christmas Seduction

**Standalone Regency romances**
Tempting the Scoundrel
Chasing the Duke

*"Love is my religion—I could die for that—I could die for you. My creed is love, and you are its only tenet."*
*- John Keats*

## CHAPTER 1

*A boisterous Derbyshire manor where neither hero nor heroine want to be...*

*December 21, 1820*

It couldn't be, but she knew it was.

Georgiana stood in a shadowed recess beneath the imperial staircase gracing Buxton Hall's entrance, a beaded reticule dangling forgotten from her wrist, her breath trapped between her lungs and her lips. The fragrances of the season—frankincense, cinnamon, roast goose—swirled, and she closed her eyes, hoping, *praying*...

But when she opened them, Dexter Reed Munro, the Marquess of Westfield, mere days from becoming the Duke of Markham if the rumor was correct, stood on the lowest step of the flight across from her, his expression amused, his head tilted as if someone had told a joke and he was considering whether to laugh.

When one *yearned* to hear that laugh.

A horde of fluttering, preening admirers surrounded him, and his smile, polite but winsome, looked so authentic they'd no idea he was soundly rejecting them. She could spot a fake right off. And, *heavens*, did she recognize the Munro brand of rejection.

*He doesn't care for society,* she'd love to tell the flock.

*He only cares for his bloody rocks.*

Georgiana released the punishing grip on her reticule, then smoothed the velvet tuft into place. With murmured appreciation, she took a glass from a passing footman and climbed the staircase opposite Dexter's, knowing they were likely to meet on the landing. Champagne bubbles erupted on her tongue, the fiery sensation giving her much-needed courage. She'd never been able to shut off the part of her that whispered *that one please* every time she came within spitting range of him. He hadn't known about her obsession, and truly, she didn't need to recall. Those untamed children racing over moor and heath, roaming the limestone caves and caverns of Derbyshire, were long gone. Their lone kiss, a glancing brush of his lips against hers before he departed on his adventures, meant nothing.

His love of fossils and stone had been the only thing he'd taken with him. The reckless, passionate sister of his closest friend, a girl who'd fallen hard during their split-second kiss, hadn't been a concern.

Thankfully, things changed. People changed.

Georgiana Whitcomb, Countess Winterbourne, was no longer reckless or passionate about anything. And with her brother's death, the circle of three friends had been forever broken.

"Markham has returned from his travels." Lady Pembroke saddled up beside Georgiana, prepared to unleash an anthology of intrusive observations.

"You're stepping ahead, my lady. For now, he's simply Westfield," she said though she didn't move away as she wished to. Lady Pembroke had a daughter, Lady Elizabeth, whom Georgiana quite liked. A review of Elizabeth's membership in the Duchess Society was going before the committee next month. The committee comprised of Georgiana and her best friend, Hildegard Templeton. Georgiana had put her heart, soul, and the experience gained from a wretched marriage—in addition to a substantial amount of her deceased husband's monies—into her organization for young ladies. Elizabeth was a prime example of a naïve girl needing tutelage on ways to navigate an aristocratic arrangement.

Ways to *survive* would be closer to the truth.

If speaking to Elizabeth's dragon of a mother was the price of admission, Georgiana was willing to pay.

Lady Pembroke tapped her fan on Georgiana's wrist, three soft rebukes. "The duke is gravely ill, or so I've heard. Westfield wouldn't have returned without a noose closing around his neck. The horrendous row he and his father had, why, it's close to six years ago as I recollect. The scoundrel cares only for things long dead and set in granite. His father, once he's dust, will finally be a person of interest."

"Closer to seven years, actually," she murmured, choosing to ignore the vulgar statement about the Duke of Markham's health. The last time Georgiana had spoken to Dex was the night of the argument with his father, where he'd been furiously packing for an expedition that would take him far from his ancestral home, far from everything, exactly as he'd wanted. Exactly as he'd gotten.

Yet, as she invariably tended to, Georgiana defended the notorious marquess, a hard, hard habit to break. "I believe geology is his profession. He didn't merely travel; the government funded his research. Surveys and such, hence the familial conflict."

Lady Pembroke grasped the walnut railing, then snatched her hand back when an evergreen needle pricked her through her glove. Holly, ivy, English fir, and mistletoe adorned every surface, framed every window until Buxton Hall looked like the forest had been invited inside the manor. "Imagine thinking to turn a hobby into a *profession*. Our set doesn't have professions, my dear. Westfield must be half-mad, as they say. Making it worse, he taught a class at Oxford last year. What future duke needs to be an academic?" She lifted a perfectly-shaped brow and brought her wounded hand before her face as if the injury puzzled her. "Childhood friends, weren't you?"

"My brother, Anthony," Georgiana said, stepping onto the landing. Even whispering his name sent her heart to shatter on the marble beneath her feet. "The marquess was my brother's closest friend."

The grief in her voice was enough to cast Lady Pembroke off like a ship that had scraped a glacier. Georgiana smiled sadly and sipped her champagne. The Ice Countess. It's what the *ton* called her, and the moniker fit. At least, it fit now that Georgiana no longer had to play a part. Play a game. She was free to do as she deemed fit.

Freedom she'd never relinquish. Not for anyone. Not for anything.

The hair on the neck of her nape lifted, cogent awareness sending goosebumps along her arms.

Georgiana glanced across the crowded landing, and there he stood.

Someone bumped into her, but the view was better from the spot she stumbled into. Between an aging viscount and an inebriated baron, both short of stature and style. Dex hadn't seen her—a temporary respite in the small space—so she seized the silent moment to record the changes. Prepare for a conversation should she have to endure one. Let the tumble her heart had taken settle in, settle down.

She palmed her quivering stomach. *Oh, my, is this feeling familiar.*

The woman at Dex's side bounced up on her toes to whisper in his ear. His smile was rueful, his lone-shouldered shrug contrite. Disarming as he brushed off the suggestion, one Georgiana didn't want to fathom. She drew an aggrieved breath through her teeth, suppressing the ridiculous, possessive burn in her chest.

However vexed she was, she couldn't deny the beauty of the moment.

Candlelight sparked off jeweled facets and polished cuff links, off the gold and silver paper looped around the banisters. Off Dex's eyes, a unique mix much like his composite rocks. Green one day, hazel the next, a surprise every time she'd gazed into them, a gift one hadn't expected to receive. He tilted his head, highlighting the auburn streaks in his hair. Not ginger, not brown but an appealing combination of both. His skin was tanned when it hadn't been before, accentuating a pale crescent scar on his temple. Slightly taller. Leaner. A hard edge shaping his face, rawness filtering into his jaw, his stubborn chin.

As it tended to, life had sculpted them both.

Surely, there were more classically handsome men, although none she'd met had the distinctive blend of intelligence and a desire for experience beyond what was easily obtained. A hunger she had as well, but she was a woman, which made all the horrendous difference in the world. A modern-day pirate minus the sword, Dex had gone through life almost incensed. And she had, from the first, *understood*.

He'd known who he was from day one, which was rare in their often counterfeit world.

Dex flicked his coat aside and braced his hand on his lean hip in exasperation, and Georgiana realized with a sinking heart that she was still attracted to him. She'd always liked the temperamental ones when the temperamental ones caused all the trouble. She'd often told the ladies of the Duchess Society: *if you have the luxury of choice, obtuse men are easier to control.*

Candlelight simply loved this clever one, she decided and polished off her champagne.

Once, so had she.

As if an ember had struck his skin, Dex glanced up and over the crowd, easily able to do so when her meager height was a hereditary disadvantage. Of course, he recognized her, his gaze sweeping low, then back. He was shocked; this was evident. His bottom lip slowly parted from the top, his eyes widening enough for her to make out the color: a dark, luscious green matching the mistletoe at his elbow. Even a hint of crimson, like the holly berries sprinkled across every table, flowed into his cheeks.

She was glad for his astonishment. Sophomorically, patently *glad*.

Because, when she turned her back and climbed the flight of stairs to the double salon, *she* was the one leaving this time.

~

It couldn't be, but he knew it was.

Dex tunneled his hand in his trouser pocket and caressed the chunk of lapis lazuli he'd found on a geological assignment in India last year. Lady Georgiana Collins—he shook his head, no, it was Whitcomb now—had eyes that color if memory served. The *ton* had gone wild over the girl, and those eyes, her first Season. Seizing on the success, her father had promptly auctioned her off to the highest bidder to save his estate. To save his arse, to be blunt. Then Anthony died. And Dex left Derbyshire, banished because he wouldn't follow his father's directive to stay and manage the duchy. Dex hadn't considered stepping in as a friend of the family, proposing a different course of action for Viscount Thimley's daughter, Georgiana. There were other men of means who'd sought an heir, a beautiful wife. Dex could have produced a list of younger, kinder candidates with scant effort.

The Earl of Winterbourne had been neither young nor kind.

Nodding to a passing acquaintance, Dex followed the crowd into the salon, memories weighing his step. It was only later, with an ounce of wisdom added to his emotional balance scale, when he'd started to miss her, miss Derbyshire like his very breath, that he recognized he hadn't been a particularly good friend. To Anthony. To her.

He'd realized a lot of things that were pointless to realize now.

Taking a standing position along the back wall with the men who expected to escape to the billiards room when the musicale began, his gaze tracked Georgiana as she smoothed her skirt and settled gracefully into one of the chairs half-circling the pianoforte. Candlelight from the chandelier washed over her as she fussed with the glass in her hand, trying to decide where to place it. Her hair was darker, honeyed wheat instead of the white blonde of their youth. Her gown was unremarkable, yet the shimmering silk clung to each gentle curve. And he'd gotten a brief look at her face. Beautiful as ever.

When everything had changed, nothing had changed.

A wave of tenderness mingled with annoyance rolled through him. Dex grabbed a tumbler from a passing footman, hardly caring what the cut crystal contained, as drinking provided pointless activity set to keep him from following the disastrous impulse to approach his deceased best friend's little sister.

He frowned, tapping his finger on the glass. Though he'd never considered Georgie a sister. His displeasure deepened. Dex took a sip of what turned out to be excellent Irish whiskey, closing his eyes to the satisfying burn. Why was he torturing himself? He'd been halfway around the world when he heard about her marriage, no way to stop what was already in motion, although his heart gave a vicious thump as it did whenever he thought of her. About Anthony. About his dying father.

Bloody, blasted Derbyshire, he seethed and tossed back the rest of his whiskey.

"Why the glower, Markham? Christmastide celebration and all. Food, spirits, music, although that forebodes to be repellant. It looks as if Lady Marshall is going to once again insist on punishing us with her talent. The pianoforte is not her friend."

Dex turned before he reconciled the look on his face. He wasn't often in polite society, and his feral edges were glinting like a blade in the sun. "It's Westfield. The duke lives."

The man at his side, a baron he'd shared a faro table with years ago at White's, took an instinctive step back. "Apologies. Word in the village is the situation at Markham Manor is dire. I simply assumed…"

Forcing his lips into a smile, Dex waved away the rest of the coxcomb's justification. "A logical conclusion. No matter. I've recently arrived from Italy, a bit short on sleep. My terseness is uncalled for. Ignore me." *Please.*

"The Ice Countess," the coxcomb whispered with a nod in Georgiana's direction. A brandy-scented dash of air slid from his lips. "Gorgeous but frightening. I wouldn't go there if I were you. Men are deathly afraid of her. And her dashed society."

Dex shifted uncomfortably, gathering others had seen where his gaze had settled. "Come again?"

The baron cocked his head, a lank of flaxen hair falling across his brow. His pale eyes lit with excitement when he grasped Dex had no idea what he was talking about. "My sister went to her school before she married. Or joined her club or whatever. The Duchess Society, the countess calls it. I don't know what she teaches because Emmaline had already attended day school or some such idiocy, but now Emma talks about a wife's rights. As if they have any. Had her husband set up a trust before she'd sign the betrothal agreement. Can you believe it?

But Patridge needed her dowry to save himself, so I guess that's his mismanagement, ain't it?"

"Indeed," Dex murmured, examining this information from all sides like he would a fossil.

Ice Countess, he thought, glancing back at her. Georgiana's head was bowed, perhaps to send the off-key musical notes over her head instead of into her ears. The nape of her neck was sleek, strands of hair escaping her chignon to curl delicately against her skin. She looked positively regal sitting there in the gilded light, the untouchable woman they imagined her to be. When the girl had been cunning, even lewd at times, intelligent to a fault, up for any challenge, any dare. Dirty hems and scraped knees and effervescent charm.

Nothing icy about her.

"I told Mother, don't send Emma to a woman who's vowed never to marry again herself. What's the use in that? Got a crusader returned to us, so I was right. As men usually are." The baron traced the toe of his patent shoe over a swirl in the Aubusson rug, a dance step with himself. "My betrothed, when I secure her, and I have my eye on a few lovely ladies, I do, because the walls are closing in on me, isn't going near any Duchess Society. No sir. I'll write that in *my* agreement."

Dex paused, holding back comment because this young buck knew little about life and even *less* about women. Never marry again? Georgiana couldn't be more than twenty-five to Dex's thirty. Undoubtedly, she had an income from her marriage, possibly a dower residence, maybe even a townhouse in the city, so she didn't have to remarry, he supposed.

But what about love, passion, children? The girl he'd known had wanted a family.

When Lady Buxton staggered into the salon carrying a massive tub of raisins soaked in brandy and asked who would not only light the dish but try to catch the flaming fruit between their teeth, Dex shoved off the wall with a frustrated oath. He'd seen the injuries resulting from this beguiling parlor trick before. "I'm done for the night. Happy Christmas," he said to the baron whose name he couldn't for the life of him recall and angled his way through the crowd, wondering why this many people wanted to spend their holiday in Derbyshire.

Wondering how he'd ended up in the same country manor as Georgiana Whitcomb.

A situation possessing dangerous potential.

Because the eager boy racing over moors and climbing towering oaks and sleeping in limestone caves was inside him, and young Dexter was tempting him, telling him to follow the inclination to halt in the salon's doorway and stare at Anthony's capricious sister until she, in turn, noticed him, a tried-and-true game they'd played before.

Which, after a hushed, pulsing trice, like a cord connected them and he'd given it a yank, she did.

He tipped his chin over his shoulder. *Meet me outside.*

Georgiana glanced at the glass in her hand, giving the crystal a firm squeeze. Then she looked back at him, her eyes *precisely* the color of the lapis wedged deep in his trouser pocket.

An earl of ill repute took the flaming raisin challenge, inadvertently setting his coat on fire. Georgiana's lips pressed as she tried not to laugh when the salon erupted in raucous shouts and absurdity. After a moment, with resignation he noted from across the room, she shrugged. *Okay.*

Dex nodded and backed into the hallway, feeling lighter than he had since coming home. Lighter than he had in years. That dangerous potential revolving like a top inside him.

Though he'd have liked to deny it, the anticipation of talking with Georgiana again sent a burst of exhilaration through him, warming him more than any whiskey could.

## CHAPTER 2

"He commands, you follow," Georgiana whispered and wiggled through the throng who'd rushed the blazing bowl of snapdragon, a drunken effort to stamp out the raisin that had set fire to not only the Earl of Piddington's sleeve but Lord Buxton's carpet.

Why, oh why, had she opted to attend this rowdy affair?

To further the Duchess Society's reach, Georgiana proposed as she exited the salon. Yet, they only tutored five young ladies at one time, and the roster was booked through 1821. *Try again, my dear.* Georgiana turned in a measured circle in the hallway, wondering where Dex had gone. Then, she noticed a path of holly berries sprinkled on parquet pine, leading away from the manor's grand staircase and into the bowels of the house. She released a hushed breath of laughter she couldn't contain. *Vexing man.*

Following the berry trail down the deserted corridor, Georgiana revised her answer. She'd accepted the invitation after making the melancholic decision to lease a home for the holiday a mere fifteen-minute ride from the Derbyshire village where she'd grown up. A ten-minute journey from her family's small estate, a house her cousin had inherited upon her father's death and not once invited her to visit.

Derbyshire was no longer hers.

The manor she'd leased was lovely. And lonely.

She was a fool for trying to step into the past.

Here she was, disconcerting decision to return aside, following a mysterious route her childhood companion had laid out like their adventures of old. Which was horrifying and intoxicating. More intoxicating than horrifying, which said a lot about how she was constructed.

The berry trail ended at the last door on the right. Georgiana paused, heart tripping, breath suspended until she forced it out with an audible puff. Why was she following Dex as she would have ten years ago?

What in the world was she doing?

She was opening the door and stepping inside what looked to be a rarely-used study—that's what. Allowing her vision to adjust to the meager moonbeams clawing through the dirty windowpanes. For a moment, she simply took it in. The gentle tick of a clock. A haunting blend of shadow and light. Furniture draped in cloth, the scent of dust and disuse, and on the lowest note, a new fragrance: man.

She was going to answer the dare, cross to the scoundrel who sat sprawled on the floor, back wedged against a threadbare sofa, long legs crossed at the ankle, two glasses, a decanter, and a flickering taper beside him. As if this was planned. As if they still knew each other. When she got closer and was able to see Dex's eyes, the color undetermined in the subdued light, she was stunned to feel her soul soaring free of her body.

His gaze, obscure at best, shouldn't have the power to turn her inside out.

Not after all this time.

He stared up at her, his delight sending tiny grooves from his eyes that hadn't been there before. "Hello, Georgie."

"Dex," she returned without a quiver, settling beside him with as much dignity as she could manage, her stomach clenching because no one had called her Georgie in *years*. She only sat because his smile was real. If he'd pulled a fake Munro on her, she would've been out of the house like a shot and back to her sorrowful manor, shimmering promise surrounding the night or not.

He nudged a glass her way with his pinkie, his aroma washing over her with the movement. Whiskey and leather and some variety of mint. He'd always smelled better than fresh biscuits, better than anything to her mind. She lifted the tumbler to her lips, her fingers trembling but not enough for him to notice. "How did you organize a private party so quickly? I'm honored."

"I raided a vacant morning room two doors down. Swiped the candle and the refreshments. I don't think they'll find us." He tipped his head to stare at the ceiling. "God, I hope not."

"You mean," she whispered against the crystal rim, "you don't find the effort to secure a flaming raisin between your teeth to be the height of amusement?"

His gaze found hers, a gradual study as potent as the brush of his finger across her skin. "Tell me something. Why the name?"

She took a slow sip, the brandy blazing a path down her throat. *Oh.* He'd heard about the society. Of course. Gossip grew like wildflowers at events such as these. "Because everyone wants to secure a duke, don't you know? Once you're Markham, you will." Her laugh was stunted, dry as kindling. "The Countess Society doesn't have the same appeal, I'm afraid. Though I'm rightly qualified."

He shifted his legs, and she tried not to notice how long they were, how his sleek black trousers clung to his muscular thighs, his lean hips. The man was built, had always been built, like a thoroughbred. "I meant the nickname, Georgie."

She swiveled around on her bottom to face him, irritation a swift tide through her veins. Blast and bother, if she showed a sliver of ankle to Dexter Munro, it was nothing he hadn't seen before. "Oh, that is *rich*. Do you know why I'm presumed to be made of ice? Because I'm financially independent and unwilling to enter into another marital agreement? No, it's my *transparency* about my situation that frightens them. I have freedom, finally, and I've made no bones about the fact I chose freedom over any other arrangement. I walk the streets alone. I ride my mount through Hyde Park as cracking fast as I like. Many women in my situation feel this way; they simply don't admit it. Or act on their liberty. It shakes the entire foundation of society. What if, they ask, we are happier *without*?"

Dex laughed, a musical sound that lit her up like one of those raisins and turned his glass in a tight circle on the floor, making a crude design in the dust. "What about passion to go with this grand liberty? A reasonable alternative for a widow of independent means to consider."

Georgiana huffed an incredulous breath through her nose and pressed her back like a ruler against the sofa. "A lover to melt the Ice Countess, you mean? You disappoint me, Dex. As if this hasn't been proposed in a hundred different ways since Arthur's death three years ago."

"By whom?" Dex asked with a brutal edge.

"Oh, don't get your hackles up, playing big brother. Although Anthony would thank you for it." She tapped her glass to his, took an insolent drink. "What I want from life is what I have. The Duchess Society and my modest circle of friends. The dilapidated dower house in Sussex where I will retire when my funds reach a level inconsistent with maintaining a middling life in London. The ability to make my own choices, good or bad, which may include tumbling off my mount during a wild ride through Hyde Park. Who knows? What I don't want is another husband. My entire life has been dictated by a man's *needs*, their mismanagement. I'm finally free to mismanage my own life, thank you very much."

Dex's head fell back, his hands going into a loose fold over his belly. "I never thought of you as a sister, Georgie."

The trilling notes of the pianoforte paraded down the hallway and slid under the crack in the door, blending with the whisper of their breaths. She'd never thought of him as a brother, so they were even.

"You're a matchmaker then?" he finally asked.

She rolled her head to find his eyes as green as the holly trimming the house and fixed on her. It was as good a time as any to admit she would always find him attractive, always experience a tug in her stomach—and a profound twist to her heart—when he was near. One had to accept what one could not change. A life lesson she'd embraced. "I educate those being forced into a situation conceivably not of their choosing. A *true* education. Many women I work with have never read a legal agreement, never managed finances or a household. In certain instances, I've arranged introductions. Call it matchmaking if you will, with suitable men who don't have vile reputations or addictions their wives would have to account for. My investigator researches every one of them, A to Z. My young ladies don't need me to teach them how to sew a straight stitch or organize a proper dinner party, although those pointless lessons are on the program to soothe anxious mothers." She looked to the moonlight streaking in the window, to the glimmers of dust sparking the air, to him. "It's what I do because I must. I teach things I wish I'd been taught."

Dex brought his hand to the bridge of his nose and squeezed, a gesture he'd employed when he had a problem he couldn't solve. "Winterbourne wasn't a good choice. With Anthony gone, I should have stepped in. I knew more about the man than your father likely did, things whispered over a gaming hell table. I should have talked to him."

"You were off with anthracite and basalt, and I, well, I made the right decision." She turned away, so she didn't have to look in his eyes during this speech. "I didn't love him. He was seventy, his life almost over, as harsh as that sounds. Arthur solved my family's financial problems without a murmur of complaint. It was a transaction. I lived mostly apart from him once he noted how often I voiced my opinions, consigned to the charming though worn dower house in Sussex I mentioned. There've been worse arrangements. He purchased a pretty vase then found he had nowhere to display it. And later, he didn't even like the vase anymore."

"Georgie…"

She shook off his pacifying plea. "I was happy being tucked away, out of sight. Honestly, I was. My independent spirit was distasteful, and I wasn't willing to relinquish it."

# THE ICE DUCHESS

She felt a tickle, turned as Dex slipped a strand of hair behind her ear. "This discussion isn't making me desirous for marriage," he said.

"Must you be desirous?" she whispered in horror as if he'd suggested he planned to take his sword and run someone through.

Dex hung his head, his spurt of laugher striking her cheek. "Oh, Georgie, how I've missed you." Heat blistered her skin as he withdrew his hand, his thumb skimming her jaw, a sensitive spot beneath her ear. He didn't linger, didn't even seem to know his touch affected her. "I must. If I don't produce an heir, my family is left with a perilous path of succession. My cousin, Alistair. Remember him? He would ravage the duchy in less than a year. Hundreds of tenant's lives held in the balance. The decision is without ambiguity, isn't it? One I've put off for far too long. When my father was still strong enough to discuss my future, I promised to provide the name of my fiancée by Twelfth Night." He tapped his fingers in a staccato rhythm on the floor. "I could hold off, perhaps, negotiate for more time, but to what purpose? It's the last thing I can give him. The last thing I *will* give him."

"So soon." The Feast of the Epiphany, Twelfth Night, was the official end of Christmastide and just over two weeks away. But the choice *wasn't* negotiable. Alistair Fontanel, Viscount Harrison, was one of the most profligate wastrels in England. A complete and utter bounder. He'd tried to kiss her when she was fifteen, and Dex had bloodied his lip in repayment. That was the last she'd seen of him. "You must marry once, I suppose. Give it a whirl," she murmured, the most inane advice she'd ever uttered.

He laughed again, the sound shadowing her like a caress. "Dependable guidance, Georgie Whitcomb."

She polished off her brandy, wishing she had more. Tomorrow, she would think about Dex marrying. But not now. Not in this enchanting world where she had his attention for the first time in seven years.

"You've visited my father," he said, the turn in conversation surprising her. "Though he didn't mention it to me."

"Of course."

"You think I'm a bad son. When I've tried, visiting Derbyshire at least once a year, managing the accounts for the estates from afar because he was ill."

She shook her head. "Maybe I think he was a bad father." At Dex's startled exhalation, she clarified, "For a man who wanted to guide his future, I mean. For a person with a life passion. He can be forgiven as it's not typical in our circle." A desire to be something more, to learn and to *know*, pieces of Dex that had wrapped silken thread around her heart and yanked tight. "He blames me, in part, for the love you have of all things deceased and captured in sediment." She released her own laugh, shocked to hear it sounded authentic. "I believe that's how he phrased it." In between coughing blood into his embroidered handkerchief.

"We were children. What to do but roam every square inch of our environs?" Dex edged his finger over until it covered one of hers, a tentative touch. The ache in her belly was immediate and overwhelming. "The fossils were a dividend to such friendship."

A burst of merriment in the hallway had them bounding to their feet. Although Georgiana was a widow and Dex a family friend, the twilight splendor of this impromptu picnic painted an intimate and vaguely improper picture neither of them could refute. There was a bump against the wall, more laughter, inebriated conversation. Georgiana grimaced, realizing they were being interrupted by a trysting couple. She looked around with a nervous giggle. The room wasn't a bad spot for it.

"Get behind the sofa," Dex whispered, adding a hand signal that looked like he was giving an order to his dog. "Under the dust cover. I'll get rid of them."

Blowing out the candle, she kicked it across the room, scrambling to do his bidding for the *second* time this evening. "How?"

"I'll figure that out when they stumble in," Dex growled and yanked the sheet over her as she dropped to a crouch, a cloud of filth raining down like snow. Not a minute later, he lifted the length of canvas just enough to catch her gaze. That look, she thought with a burst of excitement she was mad to feel—she should've been afraid of that look. That smile. His eyes had changed color, too. Always a dreadful sign. Now hazel, with dazzling, devilish streaks of gold racing through them. She'd have loved to record mood to color, a notion as crazy as the exhilaration pulsing through her.

"A wager," he whispered as the study's doorknob rattled. "Remember those?"

"Are you daft? I'm not wagering like we did when we were children!"

His smile captured his entire face. "Are you saying no to a wager? You? Georgiana Elaine Collins Whitcomb?"

She glanced at the door, where the commotion continued though no one had tumbled in on them yet. Waving her hand frantically, she said, "Yes, yes, I'm amenable!"

"The couple about to interrupt our reunion. I say it's Lady Alexander and Lord Welford."

She searched her mind for interactions she'd helplessly recorded this evening. "Lord Ambrose," she blurted. "And Lady Delmont-Burris."

"Inspired," he murmured and tapped his travel-weary Hessian on the faded carpet, pulling his bottom lip between his teeth. No silly patent heels for this man. His expression was wicked. She'd forgotten how much she liked being wicked, too. "If I win, you draw up a list of three suitables from your society." He sketched his hand in a lazy loop, nothing complimentary about her life's work in the gesture. "I need help finding a wife, and you can advertise having assisted a lowly man saddled with a dukedom. Fairly charitable my piece, as it's good for both of us. Will completely legitimize your organization's name if one pauses to consider."

She rocked back on her heels, flustered but definitely, *definitely* not overcome with jealousy. "Dex, the suitables I typically locate are *men*."

He released another of those dangerous smiles. "Not my proclivity."

"Yes, I've heard," she couldn't help but reply.

His brow winged high, just the one. A trick Dex knew made her want to punch him. Or used to. And, blast it, he'd left it to her to ask, "What do *I* get if I win?"

He gazed at her, a flurry of emotions sweeping his face. "What do you want?"

"An adventure," she answered without thinking.

The moon moved behind a cloud and shadow swept over him. "Done," he returned and dropped the sheet as the door burst open, and the amorous couple stumbled in.

In the end, she and Dex both won.

Lord Ambrose and Lord Welford made fumbling excuses for entering a deserted space when their respective spouses were in other parts of the house, while Dex made gracious asides, offering no explanation for his presence in the room, not one word. And no one asked.

After they left, Dex's footfalls closed in on her. "My, that was interesting. To be safe, stay here for ten minutes, then return to the party. I've got to get back to my father. Tomorrow, we'll discuss the wager over lunch at Markham Manor, one o'clock." With the toe of his boot, he nudged something beneath the sheet. "Merry Christmas, Georgie," he said and crossed the room, the door a soft snick behind him.

Dazed, Georgiana rooted around, brushing her hand over a round pebble. She sighed and flipped the canvas back, dust swirling and shimmering in the moonlight. The rock was a dazzling cerulean glow against her pale skin. It had been in his pocket, she surmised, as heat flowed from the stone and through her body.

*What have I gotten myself into*, she wondered as she closed her fingers around a Christmas gift only Dexter Munro would think to give her.

## CHAPTER 3

*D*ex stared out the window in his father's bedchamber, the rasp of lungs trying valiantly to draw air and mostly failing the only sound. Snow was starting to fall, the flakes drifting to the ground in ghostly swirls. This land called to him, even if he'd left in a blind panic only to return when forced. Pushed away by ambition, drawn back by obligation.

Some would be surprised to find the Marquess of Westfield loved Derbyshire more than any place he'd ever been, and he'd been many places. The rolling hills and hamlets, limestone caverns, and broad rushing rivers. The northeast quadrant where Markham Manor resided was gently mountainous, abundant in all the wondrous things that held his supreme interest. Coal, iron ore, lead, zinc, manganese, barytes. Caves layered in marble and fluorite, littered with fossils and minerals.

He couldn't imagine growing up anywhere else. *With* anyone else.

Which brought his mind back to Georgie.

He tapped his knuckle to the chilled windowpane. Those glorious cobalt eyes, the dimples that flared to life when she smiled, had led him on a merry dance this eve. He laughed and shook his head. Still susceptible to her charms. Before, she'd been too young and he a foolish boy who wasn't sure what he wanted, what he needed. He'd had much to prove, many people to *disprove*. He'd done exactly what he'd said he would, made a living, a remarkably sound one, off the hunks of sediment his father claimed would be the ruin of a five-hundred-year-old duchy, when Dex was the most proficient mining surveyor in England, his inane knowledge of rocks coveted by those willing to pay and pay well.

But ambition had exacted a personal cost, no doubt about it. Cost *her*, too, he was coming to suspect.

Bracing his arm on the wall alongside the velvet drape, he drew a breath smelling faintly of vinegar and decay. He'd never wanted to marry anyone. Truthfully, because he could be truthful in his dying father's dank bedchamber when there was no one, not even the dying father, to listen—he'd never wanted to marry anyone but *her*.

The dilemma? He wanted a wife when Georgie quite adamantly didn't want a husband.

"Impulsive fool," he whispered and bumped his forehead to the glass. How had he imagined making a reckless wager would ease the burden of seeing Georgie again, *touching* her again, and realizing he'd indeed made a grave mistake leaving her behind?

Now, she wanted adventure.

Dex glanced to the turbulent storm raging outside the window, a world of flawless, fluttering white. How to provide an adventure when the roads would be inches deep in mud and ice come morning? Travel of more than a mile or two a nightmare. If he could have taken her to the limestone caverns in Chinley, the ones they'd explored as children, shown her everything he hadn't known to show her before, things he hadn't known *how* to show her before, that would have been a start. Surely, passionate kisses surrounded by thousand-year-old quartz was an adequate quest.

A petite adventure, a beginning.

He lifted his head from the frigid pane. A beginning, not a spot mired in the middle of life, which was what his conversation with Georgie at Buxton's gathering had felt like. An unsullied *start* was what they needed, with no repulsive earls who'd turned out to be atrocious husbands or indecisive, inexperienced future dukes mucking it up. Dex had until Twelfth Night to give his father an answer. A ticking clock, as it were. Which he would do because denying a dying man's wish was an act Dex couldn't stomach.

And, frankly, he worked well under pressure.

His mind shifted to the wooden crates stacked in the Oak Room, ones he'd shipped from all over the globe the past three years. He grinned and shoved his hair from his eyes. There were adventures aplenty in those boxes if the right person was there to unpack them.

His spontaneous wager was set to put Georgie's disdain for marriage to the test.

Because he planned to tell her what he wanted in a wife, what he wanted in *life*, what he could give of his heart, mind, and soul, which was substantial. He would cheerfully review her list of suitables while he went about convincing her *she* was his only suitable.

Very politely, he would consider each one, without considering any at all.

In the process, he'd get to know her again. And she him.

Then, on Twelfth Night, Dex would find out if Georgie meant to keep him.

## CHAPTER 4

*G*iving away her coat the following morning was an easy decision to make.

Georgiana pressed the length of woven wool into Jane Fletcher's trembling hand, her own hand trembling though she tried to hide it. "Please take it. I have another at home," she said, although she didn't. But Georgiana had been unable to ignore the comments made at the Buxton's party about a family in the village with a new baby, little warm clothing, and meager supplies for the season. When she'd gone to find them, it had turned out to be a family she'd known for most of her life.

"But the ride back without a coat…" Jane gestured to the window and the angry swirl, a lank of dull brown hair dancing across her cheek with the movement.

Georgiana glanced at the bread, eggs, mutton, and vegetables sitting on the Fletcher's nicked wooden table, her bounty after a thorough raid of her manor's provisions. Knitted socks, a scarf, books, a length of chalk, a square of slate. She'd even found two apples tucked on a low pantry shelf, a surprise delighting the Fletcher children to no end. "I have a riding blanket in the carriage. A heated brick. And less than two miles to travel." She appealed again, presenting the coat. She was *not* leaving with it warming her shoulders. "I insist. My goodness, Jane, I've known you since we were children. Anthony was quite friendly with your brother, Edwin, if you recall. Oh, the trouble they used to get into!"

Jane cradled her newborn son against her chest, the babe swaddled in a faded slip of cotton, his cheeks mercifully plump and rosy with good health. Finally, with a sigh, she took the coat from Georgiana, pressed her nose into the lapel, and inhaled softly, then lovingly draped it over the chair at her side. "We miss you, my lady, we do. There's never anyone from your estate who comes to the village. Since your father died, not a word from the house on the hill. Things have fallen off the edge of a cliff, they have. The church roof is leaking, the roads pitted and unsafe. A fire at the mercantile last month, necessities for the winter dwindling."

Georgiana tied her satin bonnet strings beneath her chin. "I'm off to Markham Manor if my coachman can navigate the main road. The marquess has returned from the continent, and I've promised to visit. Perhaps I can speak to him. The duke is unwell, or surely he would have taken greater care in the village. His tenants have always spoken highly of him."

Jane's smile was beatific, a reminder of all Georgiana loved about Derbyshire and its people. She was home, even if returning felt a bit like stuffing yourself into a piece of clothing you'd long outgrown. But Sussex and London didn't fit, either.

The knock on the door had them turning in bewilderment.

"Who could that be in this tempest?" Jane asked, crossing to the cottage's modest foyer, her oldest child clutching her skirt and trailing behind.

When Jane opened the door and Georgiana saw Dex standing beneath the ramshackle portico, snow a feral flurry around him, his arms loaded with foodstuff and supplies, her breath jumped out like she'd taken a fierce thump to the back. The lapis stone he'd given her seemed to heat up from its spot in her concealed bodice pocket as if it recognized its true owner.

Georgiana stepped back as Dex stepped inside. His gaze snagged hers before circling the room and settling on Jane. Chauncey, Dex's valet since he was a boy, stumbled in behind him, his arms filled with all manner of jars and tins.

Dex delivered his donations—flour, sugar, jam, cider, ale—and gestured to the carriage parked outside. "The footman is unloading more; what I was able to gather quickly. Blankets, clothing, candles, coal, wood. Please distribute to those in need." Glancing around, he fidgeted adorably, recognizing every morsel of attention in the room was fixed on him. A flush swept his cheeks and Georgiana's body heated in response, her reaction thankfully hidden beneath layers of cotton and wool. "My majordomo was notified about an overturned coach on the main road. The countess's staff mentioned she was delivering much-needed supplies to the village when I arrived at her home. So I circled back and ransacked Markham's cupboards." He frowned and tugged a rather abused top hat from his head, his gaze drifting away as he slapped it against his thigh.

A ghost of a smile crept over Georgiana's face. Dex had been worried. An overturned carriage his concern when she'd been set to arrive at Markham Manor. So worried he'd come after her when the plan had been for her to go to him.

"My coachman is experienced with icy roadways," she murmured, just for him. "Quite knowledgeable. Lovely handle of the reins. A regular whip."

He grunted, throwing her a look both amused and discomfited. She'd never, not once in her life, seen the like with this man. Without trying, she'd knocked Dexter Munro on his muscular backside.

She wished she knew how she'd done it so she could do it again.

With a gentle nudge from Georgiana, Jane explained the dire situation in the village; Dex promised to assist, with apologies for his family's unwitting disregard. Jane was grateful, asking with genuine concern about the duke's condition, which Dex told her remained unchanged. Once the pleasantries were concluded, he bowed, popped his hat on his head, and tightened his scarf, a length of deep emerald knit exactly matching his eyes. "I must be off. I have an appointment."

Catching Georgiana's gaze, he mouthed, *with you.*

After wishing everyone a happy approaching Christmas, she and Dex stepped outside and were immediately sucked into a blinding snowstorm. Chauncey staggered to her carriage and, with a thump on the trap, set off down the lane, leaving her standing in ankle-deep slush beside Dex's luxurious conveyance.

"My coachman also has a lovely handle on the reins. And a warmer brick than yours, I'm guessing," Dex shouted over the gusts ripping between them. She shivered, unbelievably more from his penetrating regard than the storm. With a low sound of impatience, he shrugged out of his coat and slipped it on her shoulders. A multi-caped greatcoat tailored for a man of impressive size, it hung nearly to her feet.

Time suspended, heat from the worsted wool stealing through her body. Closing her eyes, she drew in his scent: leather, bergamot, man. Bringing herself back, she blinked to find his head cocked in deliberation, snowflakes sticking to his dark lashes, to the curved brim of his hat. "What's that look for?"

He released a furtive smile and assisted her into the carriage. "Nothing much. I simply think it looks better on you."

As they rolled away from the Fletcher's cottage, the wheel hit an icy patch, and Georgiana gripped the ceiling strap with a whispered oath. "Is this to be my adventure, Dex? Overturning in a Derbyshire ditch?"

He glanced over from his position across from her, shifted his long legs, the heel of his boot neatly trapping the hem of her soiled skirt. "You're the only person to call me that. I think of myself that way, too, which is odd, I suppose. And when I'm here, I feel like Dex Munro." He looked to the window, brow creasing as he retreated to his own space. "Strange when I'm not sure I know him well."

"Who do you feel like away from here?" she whispered, caught in the intimacy of the carriage's shadowy interior, the landscape of barren, milky white they traversed, the wind a shrieking moan against the sides of the conveyance. Hushed breaths and the scent of buckskin and frost, smoke from the Fletcher's hearthfire, mint, cinnamon, soap.

He didn't answer; she didn't press. Only huddled into the fragrant folds of his coat and let the motion of the carriage soothe her. They lumbered over the stone bridge crossing the River Derwent, closing in on Markham Manor. Even amid the fierce storm, she easily located the imposing dwelling nestled among vast woodlands, the rocky hills and heather moorland land she'd once known as well as her face in a mirror.

This quiet ease was one of the things she remembered about Dex's friendship, their ability to simply *be*. They'd been able to spend time together but apart, no false effort to construct a house of words. Dex with his rocks, she with her books, Anthony with his drawings. She'd never been comfortable exposing her true self in the presence of anyone else.

She sat back against the velvet squabs with an inward, private sigh, her gaze touching on Dex as he stared out the window, love and dread and regret lingering in his eyes. Heartbreaking to realize this moment was more intimate than any she'd ever shared with her deceased husband.

~

Markham Manor was haunting and magnificent. A chaotic blend of Tudor and Jacobean architectural styles, the enchanting house enthralled but did not charm—much like Dex.

With a dying duke in residence, the staff hadn't made any effort to decorate for the holiday. Servants were scarce, the hallways chilled and cheerless as if the dwelling was already in mourning. Wilkes, the butler for as long as Georgiana could remember, escorted her to the Oak Room, the oldest in the house, while Dex went to check on his father. The ever-efficient servant had tea and biscuits delivered, the fire stoked, candelabra lit, Dex's coat taken from her and hung to dry, leaving her to roam the vast space with her mood falling between anxious and eager. She gazed at the carved oak lining the walls, remembering Dex had once told her the first duke purchased the paneling from a German monastery in the 1500s.

The weight of time and age and experience hung heavy in the room. She tucked her finger in a sculpted nook, wondering what it must feel like to shoulder responsibility for this home and everyone serving it, every tenant living off the land, the village inhabitants. Quite a burden, she imagined while studying the four-hundred-year-old panels.

She poured tea, then sipped as she walked, noting how Dex had re-engineered the space for his use. Sculptures once scattered about had been relegated to a dark corner. A sketch that looked to be created by a master lay perched against the imposing mahogany desk, in its place on the wall an unframed map was tacked. Crates of varying sizes sat before the east gallery's shelves, floor to ceiling, obscuring the rows of books though the scent of leather covers and moldy pages lingered. She'd spent much time here as a child, borrowing from the library of her dreams. Running her finger over a cracked spine, she wondered what Dex had planned. The ghastly weather meant their adventure had to be conducted inside the house.

An adventure of the mind. Her favorite kind.

She'd only tagged along on the others, racing over boggy moors and exploring damp, often dreary caves, digging up fossil and stone, because Dex had asked it of her. Anthony, too. And she'd have been damned before she let them leave her behind.

She placed her teacup on the desk and traced a brand burned into one of the crates. Munro Geological. Fierce and unexpected pride swept her. Despite her secretly wishing Dex wouldn't roam so far from home to fulfill his dreams, he'd fulfilled them and then some.

He moved behind her before she realized he'd entered the room, and she went from relaxed to aware in one second.

Reaching around her, he glided his hand over a label glued to the crate. Unexpectedly and with absolute clarity, she imagined his fingers tracing words written on her skin. "We packed this one at the Messel Pit just outside Frankfurt. A bituminous shale mine abundant in fossils. Geologists are called in to safely remove the artifacts, identify and record them, then ship them back to the requested museums. So these are only mine on loan." He laughed softly, his breath streaking past her cheek, dancing inside her ear. "I try not to pilfer though I'm often tempted."

"There's much work to complete," she murmured, moving away from Dex and the teasing scent stealing into her nostrils with each breath, his heat branding her as surely as he'd branded the crates housing his artifacts. Moving away from the compulsion to turn and walk into his arms, a heedless action undermining her effort to compile a list of suitables, two names written on a folded sheet and tucked beside the lapis in her bodice pocket.

Her foolish wager, her promise to help a family friend find his duchess.

The woman who would warm Dex's bed, share his laughter and his wisdom, his stubbornness and his joy, have his children, things Georgiana had once wanted. Impossible dreams now. Her shameful marriage had ruined the chance for her to enter into an agreement like that ever again.

The Ice Countess had settled into a state of numb comfort. She couldn't wake herself. Wouldn't wake herself. Not when it had taken this long to find a glimmer of happiness. When Dexter Munro, heir to the Duke of Markham, by fate and pledge and duty, had no choice in the matter. Marry, he must. Be awake he must, while she would go on sleeping.

With a grunt, he hefted a crate atop his shoulder, the muscles in his arms, covered in nothing but a layer of fine cotton, flexing. "We'll start the adventure in Germany before moving to Denmark. For lunch, a winter picnic is called for, I think. Remember when we used to hold those in this very room? Spread out on a blanket before the fire, eating until our bellies ached. Anthony always liked those."

A picnic. With Dex. In her favorite room in the house. With her favorite *person* on the planet. "I'm to help you categorize your pieces then?" she asked breathlessly, turning the conversation to a topic she could manage, her heart plummeting to her knees.

He paused halfway across the room, tipped a grin at her. "If you wouldn't mind. I need to note the scientific names for each, but my spelling is appalling. As I recall, you were exceptionally talented in Latin when it was bollocks to me. I'm happy to provide amusing, even embarrassing, tales of how I acquired each piece."

She shrugged, dusting her damp boot through the dust on the floor. Markman Manor needed a woman's touch and better supervision of the servants, she concluded, reminding her of the blasted list in her pocket. Someone experienced in household management mentally added to the future-duchess wish list. "Father was generous in allowing me to sit with Anthony's language tutor. I can make notes for you. Be your assistant today, should you need one."

He wrestled the crate to the floor and dropped to his haunches beside it. "Exactly what I need," he murmured so quietly she almost missed it. Reaching beneath the desk, he slid a crowbar out. "This spot is the keyhole to the kingdom," he said and jammed the thin metal edge between a gap in the wood, and with a violent twist, sent the crate's lid tumbling.

She got lost watching him unpack his treasures, separating each parcel from straw with reverent handling and mumbled observations she had no idea how to interpret. Beautiful hands, sleek wrists, a dusting of dark hair climbing into his rolled sleeve. Broad shoulders, wide chest, lean hips, long legs, he was built like a man who used his body. He should've looked disheveled, snow-moist and mussed, covered in grime and bits of straw, when instead he looked utterly appealing. The lit taper on the desk highlighting the auburn streaks in his hair, flooding his eyes with sparks of light. Eyes full of captivation and delight over his possessions.

She went to her knee beside him, fascinated because he was. He'd laid the fossils in a neat line on a length of tarp. "This one," she pointed, fearing to touch, "has color."

Dex smiled, tapping the fossil she'd pointed to. "A jewel beetle. The pigment is the exoskeleton showing. Quite unique, that. Buprestidae, which I can say but not spell. Which is where you come in." He made a motion as if to write, his smile growing.

"Oh!" She scampered to her feet, having forgotten about playing assistant geologist.

"My folio is on the desk. A sharpened quill. Fresh ink. Notecards we can attach to each specimen. Twine and scissors."

"You're prepared," she said, gathering the materials.

"I'm a man of science. I like details. I like strategizing." He unpacked the last specimen and shoved the crate aside. "You should also know this about me. Once I get an idea in my mind, it rarely leaves. And more than anything, I like to win."

Georgiana paused, dabbing at a smear of ink on her palm. "So, you're stubborn and competitive. You didn't have to tell me, those traits I recall," she said dryly and dropped to a squat, placing the materials in a row as neat as his line of fossils. "Are we fighting? With talk of winning and such."

"Sometimes winning has nothing to do with fighting, Georgie girl," he returned with an enigmatic expression. Then he shook his head as if amused by them both, sending his hair in a wild tumble about his face.

She moved before she thought to stop herself, brushing the overlong strands from his eyes. They were the color of burnt honey against her skin. Lingering, she let her fingers graze his temple, his cheek, the underside of his jaw. "No need to hide that face," she said as they stared, knees touching, breath mingling. His skin smelled like winter. Charred wood and damp frost and cool sunlight. Stunned, she laughed and dropped her hand, making light of the action when her awareness had constricted to a pinpoint of sensation sitting right beneath her heart.

Silent but vigilant, Dex blinked, reached for the scissors, snipped a length of twine, and turned, presenting his back and the cord. "Tie it. It's what I do when it's gotten too long, and I'm without a barber. I'll have Chauncey trim it later. He has a steady hand when the situation calls for one, which in the remote places we've traveled, it often has."

"I'm guessing you're the only geologist who travels with a valet."

"Quite right." He dipped his head, patient, controlled, *persistent*. His request felt like a dare, an intimate and personal one. A task a wife completed for her husband, a woman for her lover. Georgiana lifted her hand, watched it tremble. Pulled her fingers into a tight fist, released, then sank them into his hair. Thick, silken, as she'd imagined. Breathing in his scent, she placed the twine between her teeth, using her other hand to gather the strands into a neat bind.

His hand went to the rug, fingers spread as he braced himself. A raw gasp snaked through his teeth, she heard it, and he made no effort to keep her from hearing it. His shoulders lifted, his biceps hardening with the effort. Parts of her body that had lain dormant for years aroused with his choked breath. He was affected; she was overwhelmed. If Dex turned, pushed her to the floor, and climbed atop her, she'd let him. Welcome him, despite her fragile heart, despite her fears, despite her suspicion that their chance at love had passed.

This level of desire was a creature she'd never experienced nor soothed.

Soothing desire wasn't what she was here for.

Swallowing, she rocked back on her heels. Tucked her finger in her bodice pocket and worked the suitables list free. It was a hammer blow of a response, nothing subtle about it, panic driving the undertaking. The lapis stone he'd given her escaped with the list and tumbled to the floor, landing right by the toe of his dirty boot. Her cheeks lit, her palms going damp. *Just bloody perfect.*

Slowly, carefully, Dex covered the stone with his hand.

"I drafted a list," she said, her words tripping one over the other. "Two women I feel are appropriate. And immediately available. The families are in Derbyshire for the holiday, and both are in dire need of funds, meaning they will happily forego the Season, which is convenient given your promise to provide a name to your father by Twelfth Night. I'm happy to hold an intimate dinner party at my home since your father is ill. I'm a family friend, a widow of means. Therefore this is entirely proper. If you have more flexibility with regard to time, I'll confer with my partner in the Duchess Society upon my return to London and—"

"*Enough,*" he whispered, a thousand sentiments wrapped in the plea. Anger, when she had no idea why he was angry. Disappointment, frustration.

Georgiana's temper flared, relieving a little of the yearning pulsing beneath her skin. How *dare* he, when she'd done nothing but what he'd asked of her. "Why do you sound vexed when I'm simply doing what you requested I do? What I've been doing quite successfully for going on two years within every level of society. We'll need to go over my suggestions if you're able to hold a civil discussion about your quest because I don't understand what you want, what you *need* in a wife. I usually conduct a thorough interview with both parties; consequently, these were *guesses*. Maybe you've forgotten, but I don't know you anymore."

He ran the lapis along his lower lip, then sent her an inscrutable look over his shoulder. "Would you like to, Georgie?" He tossed the stone from hand to hand. "Know me again?"

A stunned sigh left her, and she spoke without thinking, "I've given up on that."

He frowned, sending a neat fold between his brows, the stone falling still in his hand. "Given up on what?"

"Friendship. Belonging. Derbyshire." She blew out a breath, unable to articulate what she meant, what she wanted, what she dreaded, what she *feared*. Funny, when she'd asked him to tell her these things about himself. "I don't know. All of this. I've been alone for so long I'm used to it. Coming back here has been like the first sweep of sunlight after winter. Addictive and startling. And in a way, uncomfortable. I'm having trouble seeing through the glare."

Didn't he know?

She was made of ice and wasn't sure she wanted to melt.

Shaking his head, Dex pulled his bottom lip between his teeth, seeming to realize a task he'd assumed would be easy wasn't going to be easy at all. "You've always had my friendship." Turning to face her, he unwrapped her clenched fist, dropped the lapis into her palm, and sealed her fingers around it. "It's entirely my fault you felt you lost it. And we must start somewhere."

"Start what?" she whispered, a tendril of unease threading through her voice.

He rose, looking down at her for a charged moment. "I'll go over your list of suitables, Georgie. Share my vision for the perfect duchess."

"I never promised per—"

"But first, we're going to have an adventure. The best I could construct in the middle of a snowstorm. As I mentioned, we'll start with travel to Germany and Austria," he said, crossing the room to the map tacked on the wall. He tapped India with his knuckle. "Maybe, before luncheon, we'll even dip our toe into Asia. Then, over whatever delicacies my kitchen staff is inspired to provide for us, I'll tell you about the fever in Delhi that nearly killed me, the viscount's daughter in Shanghai who brandished a knife and thought to force my hand, my plans to survey parts of Scotland and Wales for a government initiative, which would keep me closer to home for the next year or two. My hopes for Munro Geological and how I pray my plans align with my duty to the dukedom. I'll tell you why I left Derbyshire, why I felt I had to. You want to know me, know me. But I get the same in return. Discussions, like we had as children."

"Dex, when we were children, when we were friends, we talked about everything."

He shrugged and tapped the map again, closer to home this time. "Okay."

She squeezed the lapis, pressing a rough edge into her skin. "You don't fight fairly," she said, soundly defeated and utterly euphoric, proving she was, indeed, losing her mind.

He laughed, shaking the neat snatch of hair tied with twine. "When you used to fight dirty. I took more than one fist to the face as I recall. A boot kick to the shins. Where is that courageous hellion, I wonder?"

*She's right here*, Georgiana wanted to say, *hiding beneath the Ice Countess.*

Instead, she slipped the lapis in her pocket, settled Dex's folio on her knees, dipped the quill, and wrote *Buprestidae* in neat script on the page. She swept the feathered end over the glowing beetle fossil. "Let's start with this one, shall we?"

His only reply was a brilliant smile and a teasing wink as he settled in beside her.

And she realized she was in deep trouble.

## CHAPTER 5

*Friend.*

Dex rolled on to his back before the hearth, the glass of whiskey he'd devoured during his late luncheon with Georgie—and the second he was diligently consuming—giving him a lovely internal glow. He steadied the tumbler on his belly and turned his head toward the brocade settee where she lay sleeping.

Her flaxen hair had come loose from its mooring and was scattered about her face. Her hand was curled in a tight fist, her cheek resting atop it. Lips, very tempting ones he'd spent much of the morning staring at, parted with the lightest, most delicate breaths slipping free. Her breasts had done a suggestive gravitational shift against her rounded bodice, bringing a new level of discomfort to the afternoon, evidence of which he'd struggled to hide from the serving maid, Gertrude, who sat snoring in an armchair in the corner. A nod to decorum his majordomo, Wilkes, on staff since Dex was a boy, had insisted upon with an impermeable scowl.

When Wilkes looked at Georgie, he saw the girl with a ragged hem and skinned elbows who'd requested he not tell her father she'd been climbing the elm out back or wading through water in a limestone cave or riding a horse astride.

Dex saw her in that way, too. In part. At times.

But mostly this day, he'd seen a woman looking back at him with the girl's eyes. The worst possible mix. The girl he'd loved and the woman he wanted.

The worst possible mix was going to be furious.

Because he *didn't* play fair.

He'd plied her with wine while explaining the stratification of igneous rock, sending her into a dispassionate, foxed trance. Because he'd known if he waited another hour, maybe two, they couldn't safely travel the roads. The snowstorm beyond the library window was positively ferocious.

She was here to stay at least until tomorrow.

His time was running out, therefore he'd had to make a move, and Dexter Munro didn't fear making moves.

Georgie wanted to host a dinner party to help him find a duchess.

*Tomorrow.*

Which left one day to either change her mind or change his.

Propping his arm beneath his head, he took a measured sip as the candlelight shifted and washed over her. Even with the lure of a dukedom, a pleasing face, a fast wit, and a sly charm, he wasn't especially adept with women. With relationships. He was skilled in bed; he appreciated the mechanics of the act. He was a man of detail, after all. And concern with detail was what it took to be competent, a technique he assumed most men ignored. From the comments from his former lovers, was sure they ignored.

Sex was one thing.

Talking and laughing and remembering like he'd done with Georgie today, as she made notes in his folio, dripping ink on the rug and asking probing, wide-eyed questions, her gaze lighting him up and then dancing off, was nothing he'd ever experienced. He was used to conversation with an end goal. A game being played, a transaction being enacted.

This had been conversation held simply to enhance their understanding of each other.

It had made him feel vulnerable, naked, panicked.

He *liked* her. He'd always liked her. She was intelligent. Beautiful. Spirited. She quarreled with him without worrying about her disagreement hurting his feelings or her chances. He believed her. She was sincere. She told him when he was daft or arrogant or obnoxious, which he often was.

But he'd boxed himself in with this suitables agreement, a dare made in haste and one he wished to retract. Impulsivity had brought him low before. This wouldn't be the first time. He couldn't very well say, *I love you and I always have*. And not in the courteous way you've outlined for us. *Friends*. With a sneer, he threw back the rest of his whiskey.

The admission sounded crass, too sudden. Reckless. She wouldn't believe it—and who could blame her? He'd have to go through with this farce to find a duchess to make the woman he wanted to *be* his duchess realize she had feelings for him, too. That she wanted him more than her damned freedom, which he had no urge, no intention, of taking from her. His only chance to secure her love was to make her jealous of the plan she'd put in motion.

In essence, having her sabotage her own creation.

If he followed through on his impulse to touch her, it might go badly. Cause her to push him away. Forever away. Opposite of future-duchess away.

He could always be honest and court her. Tenderly, for months if necessary. Tell his father by Twelfth Night that he'd proposed, and they would marry when Georgie was *ready* to marry. But instinct, a gift that rarely failed him, told Dex her issues were more profound than merely losing her independence. His fingers clenched around the glass as he released a tense breath. The notion sent a flood of rage through him, but he suspected Georgie's marriage had broken her. Leaving Dex to tame a hesitant filly when horses didn't particularly fancy him.

When patience wasn't his strong suit.

Placing his tumbler aside, he rolled to his feet and quietly approached the settee. Went down on one knee next to Georgie, close enough to catch the scent of lavender and nutmeg on her skin. Close enough to see the line of freckles scattered like stars across the bridge of her nose, the smudge of ink on her jaw. Suddenly, he wondered what she thought of him. Because her feelings weren't obvious. He'd always known before, but the Ice Countess had become adept at concealment.

He wondered if her heart raced when he touched her. If her mind emptied when he smiled. If she wanted him in the core of her being, an inexplicable *ache*.

But most of all, he wondered if she remembered their kiss.

He scrubbed his hand over his jaw, stubble pricking his fingertips. Drawing a breath filled with her, he closed his eyes to the memory. It was years ago, seven or eight now that he tried to place it. He'd been in his father's study packing papers for his first geological assignment after finishing Cambridge, an archaeological dig in Italy. He was coming off a violent confrontation with the duke about, well, everything when Georgie had stumbled in.

Dex had been a churn of emotion. Tangled up. Exposed. Infuriated and eager and bloody scared. Then she'd been standing before him, her face flushed, her eyes shimmering. He hadn't told her he was leaving, but Anthony must have. The next moments were hazy. He couldn't recall what they'd said to each other. What she'd done to make him reach for her, drag her up on her toes and against his body.

But the kiss, oh, how he remembered the kiss.

Nothing transactional about it. Pure, sweet, flawless. Innocent for all the heat it had sent through him. An awakening, even if he still walked away from her, from Derbyshire, the next morning.

An honest mistake. Young and foolish, he hadn't known.

He'd let the only woman he'd ever want, ever *love*, marry someone else.

"Dex."

He opened his eyes to find Georgie blinking sleepily. She yawned behind her hand, giving him a pointed look. "You mustn't mix discussions of igneous rock and wine. It's a disastrous combination."

Dipping his head as he laughed, he braced his hands on his knees to keep from touching her. *Measured steps, Dex, my boy, measured steps.* "Duly noted."

She elbowed to a sit, smoothing her bodice and her skirt while he glanced away to give her privacy. "Did you do this on purpose? Provide spirits and deadly conversation." She nodded to the window and the snowdrift climbing past the bottom panes. "I'm stuck here, aren't I?"

The delicate hollow of her throat was within reach should he follow through on the desire to press his lips to it. Which, as he was unsure of himself *and* her, he wouldn't. "My father's sleeping and the doctor doesn't expect him to wake," he shocked the hell out of himself by admitting. "I suppose…I suppose I didn't want to spend the day alone."

"The unfair play continues," she whispered and worked a loose tendril of hair behind her ear, "as I can say nothing to that."

"You have a chaperone," he reminded her with a nod to Gertrude, who'd been equally felled by the stratification discussion and slept as soundly as a babe. "A houseful of servants. Wilkes has popped his head in every half-hour since you arrived. I don't know what he thinks I'm doing to you in here. Each time, he seems surprised to find out, *nothing*."

A devilish spark lit her eyes, reminding him of the indigo of the Indian Ocean. There were leagues of mysteries in her gaze. Couldn't he be the one allowed to explore them? "What trouble can two old friends get into surrounded by a slumbering chaperone, an aging butler, and twenty crates of rocks?" She clicked her tongue against her teeth and glanced about the room. "A note for the future wooing of your duchess: fossils aren't romantic. Fascinating but not romantic."

A burst of well-concealed frustration vibrated through him. What trouble indeed. He could think of *lots*. "I agree with your earlier suggestion. Let's start tomorrow. Here. The suitables. *I'll* host the dinner party. There's no time like the present, and even with scant notice and snow a sodding foot deep, no one will refuse an almost-duke. Or the chance to be an almost-duchess. I'll send my best carriage for them and pray the roads are passable. Formal livery, every opportunity to impress. Even such a simple gesture, your assisting me with this endeavor, will be a boon for the Duchess Society, am I correct?"

She looked back, surprised, conceivably a bit stunned.

It wasn't jealousy, but it was a start.

"Twelfth Night, Georgie, remember? I made a promise to my father, and I mean to keep it." He tapped the timepiece lodged in his waistcoat pocket. "Tick, tick, tick."

She dragged her thumbnail over her bottom lip, and memories of their long-ago kiss roared through his mind. Helping to relieve his pent-up frustration, she was *not*.

"No time like the present," she echoed. "They're lovely, the two young ladies I hope to introduce you to. Accomplished. Demure. Entirely appropriate."

"Listed in *Debrett's*."

She cocked her head, trying to decipher his tone. "Well, yes, of course. As *we* are. You say it like it's a stain." Irritation crossed her lovely face. "You sound less than enthusiastic when this was your idea. I'm helping because *you* need it."

With a sigh, he rose to his feet. "Darling Georgie, I sound resigned."

"Rocks and resignation aren't going to secure a duchess, Dex."

"How about my charming personality? Will that do it?"

She tapped her boot heel against the settee in serious consideration, as if this wasn't likely to secure any duchesses either.

He frowned, stung. "I can be charming, you know. And if I can't, the title will secure any knot I chose to tie. It holds the allure I lack."

"When surrounded by mounds of dirt and pickaxes, I'm sure you can be charming."

"Are you saying I've lost my Town bronze? That's a bloody compliment."

She stood, her gaze locked on his. Petite, which he'd forgotten over time, the top of her head barely reaching his shoulder. He wanted to tuck her against his body and never let her go. Protect them both from the coming storm. "Your rough edges make you interesting, Dex, in a sea of people who aren't. They always have. The goal is to find the woman who will appreciate them."

*Okay.* His shoulders relaxed, a quick gust of air leaving his lips. Georgie liked his rough edges, which at this point were there to stay. "Then you'll help me find her?"

Her finger charted the line of her jaw, her cheek, as she swept a lock of hair behind her ear. He followed the motion, enthralled, certain he'd not desired a woman more in his entire bloody life. "I'll help you find her."

Dex crossed to the window to hide his body's ferocious reaction. The stretch of Derbyshire he viewed from the window was an ivory blanket unfurling to the horizon, broken only by a pointed mountain peak piercing the low-hanging mist. Nothing was more beautiful than winter here, nothing except the woman standing across the room from him, caught as he was between friendship and regret. He'd made a hash of things for years, and it seemed unlikely anyone would grant him a Christmas miracle.

For his father, for Georgie.

He'd been given no advice and certainly had no wisdom concerning love. His father had been a harsh taskmaster, reserved and unreachable, his mother deceased by his fifth birthday, his childhood, except for Anthony and Georgie, solitary. Science had been the center of his universe, and he'd clung to it gratefully.

Love, he knew nothing about.

In any case, why wish for a miracle when he wasn't sure he believed in them?

Behind him, Dex heard Georgie unpacking another crate as she hummed quietly beneath her breath, an action he wasn't even sure she realized she was doing. She was a competent assistant, shaving hours off the tedious administrative work that was a large part of his research. They worked well together, which meant *something*, didn't it?

He tapped the frigid windowpane with a tender smile as he contemplated miracles. Being with Georgie for another day was a minor one now, wasn't it?

## CHAPTER 6

*A*s conversation traversed the softly lit dining room, none of the participants suspected Georgiana had stayed the previous night in a guest bedchamber three doors down from the Duke of Markham's heir. A luxurious space she'd roamed until dawn for reasons more troubling than the game Dex was playing.

Three doors between her and the man she was trying diligently if halfheartedly to find a proper duchess for.

Georgiana glanced at Dex from the corner of her eye, wondering at his mood. Sardonic charm on display, not exactly what he'd promised. Except for a blinding white cravat that only served to highlight his sun-kissed skin, he was dressed in formal obscurity from head to toe. A look both careless and cavalier. Thankfully, the clack of silver against china and an abundance of wine had polished the rough edges off the evening if not the man. The setting was lovely, befitting a marquess-cum-duke. Cinnamon, clove, and ginger lingered delightfully in the air, the table was awash in candlelight spilling over ropes of holly, a feast of food, merriment, drink. Servants scurried and bowed, giggling and a little haphazard, again making Georgie think firm guidance at Markham Manor would benefit everyone.

Due to the weather, they'd only been able to secure the attendance of one family this eve, news Dex had taken without glancing away from his fossils, making Georgiana question if she worried more about finding a duchess than he did.

"Westfield, you must tell us about your adventures. I hear you spent time in India. Always wanted to go myself," James Hightower, the Earl of Atherton said around a burp he tried politely to cloak. He was in the process of bartering his eldest daughter to temper his graceless business decisions, and Georgiana was having trouble overlooking this fact. Sophia Hightower was another helpless young woman placed in a precarious position by someone who should have sought only to protect her. The need for a sudden influx of capital brought about reckless decision-making. Georgiana should know, as she'd once been a pawn in a brutal arrangement. She understood she'd never be able to accept these situations less than personally, which was a weakness of character but critical for heartfelt management of the Duchess Society.

"Bombay the most recent. India is..." Dex's reckoning gaze circled the room and landed on her. "Intoxicating. An explosion of color and scent. And taste. Extreme poverty and glorious wealth an amalgam on every street until you're dazed from walking them. It's exhausting and magnificent. A place in the world one should experience."

Georgiana glanced down, moving peas in a circle on her plate. Forget Dex's passionate words. His eyes held reflective meaning, sizzling with emotion and eager appeal, nothing he directed toward the eligible woman sitting two seats away from him. *No*, he wasn't going to make it that easy. He'd been tossing Georgiana hot looks all night; her stomach was tangled in a knot from trying to ignore them.

"You'll leave the geology nonsense behind when you gain the dukedom, am I right? Take up hunting or horse racing. Carriage driving seems a fine sport, very fine. No need to go haring back to Asia or some such," the earl said with a pat to his round belly, as if Dex's work was less than trivial. "Not when London, and secondly, Derbyshire, are enough, more than, for any man."

"Hmm, give up my rocks..." Dex took a languid sip, and her heart thumped to note his eyes gleaming a feral lime green, a color that had signaled a brewing battle when they were children. "What do you think, Lady Sophia, about a man abandoning his profession? His lone fixation since he found his first fossil, oh, at seven or eight years of age. His obsession, as it were, in a world where many stumble through life without one."

Georgiana raised her wineglass to her lips, the sip more a gulp and vastly essential to her surviving this dinner. Dear God, Dex was a caged tiger set loose on society. She should have recalled his obstinacy, his unyielding view of life, and his purpose within it.

Sophia, all of nineteen and preparing for her first Season, blinked while adjusting her spectacles, which were charming but regrettable if she truly needed them. "If I had such a pursuit, my lord, one near to my heart, I wouldn't forsake it for anything," she said with only a faint tremor. Then she promptly sent her gaze to her plate of roast goose as if it was the most interesting thing in the room.

The smile Dex bestowed, not one of his fakes, took Georgiana's breath away though it had little effect on Sophia when the girl glanced up and found it.

"You don't mean that dearest," Countess Atherton murmured from across the table.

"I do," Sophia answered in a dogged tone Georgiana was beginning to believe spelled trouble. "You know I do."

The earl set his glass on the table with a thunk. "We talked about this. It's preposterous."

Dex caught Georgiana's eye. *Brilliant*, he mouthed, the effort to repress his smile nearly cracking his cheeks.

With a sigh, Georgiana polished off her wine, tempted to smash her glass over his head.

Sophia turned to Dex and gave her spectacles another shove. "My lord, may I be so bold as to admit I cannot yet marry, should this be the reason for this agreeable banquet. I need more life experience for the page. Like Miss Austen, I'm compelled to write." With an edgy exhalation, she rushed to add, "Composing stories is my passion. My *only* passion."

"I never mentioned passion," Dex whispered for Georgiana alone.

She could only think that when this dinner party was over, she might strangle him.

In the end, the evening was a congenial disaster, the earl and countess making every attempt to confirm they'd had an enjoyable time and would love to entertain when they were next in Derbyshire. Atherton pulled Dex aside, and Georgiana imagined he was making a plea to keep his daughter's unconventional comments forever within the confines of Markham Manor. The countess pulled Georgiana aside and petitioned for her daughter's acceptance into the Duchess Society, which Georgiana, after getting a first-hand look at Sophia's mettle and naïve charm, agreed to secure.

A beautiful, young bluestocking? Georgiana wasn't about to see such a spirited independent thrown to the wolves.

"I'm sorry your dinner didn't go as planned," Dex said when he returned from escorting his guests out to find Georgiana slumped on the bottom step of the sweeping central staircase, her head in her hands. "Although it was more entertaining than Drury Lane, regretful to admit. The last play I attended there was ghastly. Tonight, I actually had a pleasant evening."

"If you laugh right now, Dexter Munro, I can't account for what I may do."

"I'm not going to laugh," he murmured and sat on the stair above her, on the opposite side, out of reach, out of touch. But she *felt* him as if he wore a hearthfire like a cloak.

She rolled her head to look at him. "If you need this, Dex, a duchess by Twelfth Night, why aren't you taking it seriously? Why don't you seem to care?"

Shrugging from his coat, he folded it in a neat bundle and laid it over the glossy walnut handrail. Bracing his elbows on his knees, he bowed his head. Georgiana brought her hands into fists to keep from brushing his hair from his brow. Sweeping the tousled strands aside, pressing her lips to the tantalizing curve between neck and shoulder. He looked like he'd set himself on an island far from everyone, although he looked comfortable, as if his aloneness were a familiar companion. "I'm having trouble"—he linked his hands, those slim, elegant fingers curling in on each other—"connecting this life to the other. The bloody title, nothing effortless about the duty imposed, and the universal expectation I should feel emotionally attached to it. Instantly and without dispute. Instead, I feel..." He shrugged one broad shoulder. "Detached from even my dying father sleeping in his bedchamber a floor above. Nostalgia has a bite, capable of injury, I'm finding. When I was here before, I suppressed my desires to manage expectations and now find I can't articulate who I truly am."

"Wreckage," she whispered, and his gaze jumped to hers, his expression fierce. She knew what it was to close oneself off only to find you'd *become* the closed-off person. "You could wait to uphold your promise to your father. The Season will provide every opportunity to find her."

"I don't want to wait," he snapped, staring at his hands.

Georgiana exhaled softly, realizing she was dealing with tender feelings, gratified Dex was showing them to her even if he wished he hadn't. "Care to tell me what's bothering you?"

He shook his head. "Not yet."

Georgiana traced the toe of her boot along a nick on the stair. "I'm sorry about Lady Sophia. I don't know her well as there wasn't time for a thorough interview, something I always conduct. This issue, her chosen profession, would have surfaced during our discussion, I feel sure."

"An agreement with Atherton would have been a fine business arrangement," he said in a jagged tone. "A unique girl beneath the stammering blushes, which is unfortunately what no man in the *ton* wants. I admire her audacity, but I can't imagine, not for one moment, kissing her. Laying a finger on her person. Isn't gaining an heir a major objective in this muddle?"

Georgiana closed her eyes, took a shallow breath. "Most marriages are not built or based on..." She fluttered her hand helplessly.

"Desire. Is that the word you're looking for?"

She opened her eyes to find his gaze fixed on her, a challenge in their hazel depths. "Intimacy, Dex. *Attraction*. It isn't as if those typically arrive with the marital contract. You know this. Part of my mission with the society is to prepare women for this deficiency. Create a protected situation within what is nothing more than, yes, a business arrangement, where both parties have enough knowledge to run the business. We don't talk about passion." Her unease, her sense of quickly losing her footing, drew her lips down. "I don't know that I've ever seen a love match represented. Only in fairy tales."

He moved quietly, deliberately, sliding across the stair until he reached her. One hand framed her face, then the other as he brought her lips to his. Soft, gentle, a whisper when other men shouted. With a silky murmur, their kiss from years ago blended with this one until she was unable to separate them. When she melted into him, her lips parting, tasting mint and wine, he pulled back, this movement *not* measured.

Embarrassed, she glanced away, wondering if she'd done something wrong. When, obviously, she'd done something wrong. Arthur had said her skills were sadly lacking, and she'd believed him.

That's why he'd had to resort to other measures.

"Look at me, Georgie," Dex said in a hard voice, though he didn't try to touch her again.

After a long, searching moment, she did. His cheeks were flushed, his breath ragged. Had she done that to him? Was it possible he wanted her as much as she wanted him?

"I realize there wasn't love involved, but did Arthur not pleasure you?"

*What to say*, her brain screamed? What to *admit*?

"He was cruel. I was untried. Amateurish. And then uninterested," she whispered even as heat began to pool between her thighs. She'd never experienced this warmth before, never imagined its existence. But Dex's fevered gaze was ripping her apart, bringing all kinds of unwanted sensations. He was ruining her with that look. "I didn't know, I couldn't make—"

He leaned and placed his lips to the base of her throat, blew a warm breath over moist skin. Delicate, like a butterfly's wings as he moved to a spot below her ear, drawing her skin between his teeth, rougher contact. Her head fell back, her lids drifting low. He charted a gradual course up her spine, his touch imprinted on each peak and hollow, a scalding press ending when he curled his hand around the nape of her neck and tangled his fingers in her hair.

Arousing beyond measure when he'd yet to truly kiss her.

The discreet cough came from the depths of the shadowed entranceway, where Georgiana spotted a footman rocking from side to side and wringing his hands, likely having stumbled on a situation he'd not before encountered, in this house at least. A draft of glacial air had come in with the boy to swirl around their feet. "Countess Winterbourne's carriage is ready, my lord," he stammered before slipping out the door into the welcoming winter.

Dex cursed, sliding back to the other side of the step, each point of contact on her body he'd breached alive with a thrumming pulse. "If I admitted you have me trapped in the palm of your hand..." Yanking his through his hair and sending it into further disarray, he blew a scornful breath through his nose. "That you could make a list of what you want to know, what you want to *do*, how to touch me, how I should touch you, and I'll eagerly strike off each until this deficiency you feel you have, which was a deficiency on Arthur's part I must tell you, is a memory of the past, what would you say?"

She stared sightlessly at her feet, leaned to polish a scuff on her boot, his words tumbling like water over a cliff inside her. "I'd say you should remember your Twelfth Night promise to your father." When Dex reached for her, she rose unsteadily to her feet. "I don't want to be a duchess," she whispered in a raw voice. A panicked admission, discourteous and hurtful, one she wished she could recant but it was too late.

Too late for a lot of things.

His gaze when it found hers, because she looked back and let herself be found, was a scorching, emotional blend. "That works because I don't want to be a bloody duke." He boosted himself from the step, yanked his coat from the banister, and dropped it to her shoulders with more purpose than care. "I'll see you out."

"You're vexed with me," she said, tugging the lapels close to her cheek. The deep breath to capture the masculine scent hidden in the woolen folds was unnecessary as it lived in her memory alongside the second kiss in her life he'd gifted her. She would take the last twenty-four hours to her grave, an experience to top all others. Tears pricked her eyes to imagine anything better than being with Dex again, the brief return of her childhood. Only Anthony sharing this time with them could have increased its appeal.

Dex opened the door and waited wearily for her to step through it. "I'm vexed with the world, Georgie. But never fear, I'll get over it."

He didn't try to stop her as she made her way down the stone steps, assisting with a light grip on her elbow to keep her from slipping, his touch restrained, his manner polite but distant. He'd gone back to his island, and she might not see him leave it. She turned as she was climbing into the carriage. "Dex, the other young lady I planned to introduce you to..."

His gaze shot to a window high above them. His father's bedchamber, she assumed. Stepping back, his hands dove into his trouser pockets as his lips flattened. "Send me a note with the date and time, and I'll be there. Looking very ducal and pretending to feel happy about this process. No one will have any clue it's *you* I want."

With this astounding statement released to the cosmos, he slapped the roof of the carriage and turned without another word, leaving her staring out into the starlit nightfall, her wishes, her feelings, in utter disarray.

∼

His rash declaration a short hour ago rolled through his mind.

*That you could make a list of what you want to know, what you want to do, how to touch me, how I should touch you, and I'll eagerly strike each off...*

He lifted the glass to his lips, certain his decision to dive into a brandy bottle following Georgie's departure would solve no problems, although it was taking the sting out of the evening's closure. In the distance, thunder rumbled, and the acrid scent of an approaching storm churned and sizzled. He smelled burning pine and, somehow, *her*. Which was impossible as he sat on Markham Manor's stone steps in a puddle of slush that had chilled until he could no longer feel his buttocks.

He wanted to be nothing but part of the night, silent from the roar in his mind, the ache in his heart. He wanted neither dukedom nor love, messy entanglements, childhood affection traps, eyes the color of lapis, the tug of slim fingers through his hair, lips that felt familiar but should not, or the weight of despair over a pledge he should have made years ago and hadn't the courage to.

He'd mucked up everything.

He'd known Georgie had an attachment to him when they were children, though he'd considered it infatuation. Charming, until he started to return the sentiment.

And now...she didn't want a husband, feared taking a lover.

Did he want to be simply an experience even if he persuaded her? Her teacher in lovemaking but nothing more, which did make his cock twitch to envision, he wasn't denying.

He shuddered, the glass quaking in his hands. One more minute of this excruciating bliss, then he'd return to the house before he expired from the cold. Check on his father, whisper words of encouragement and promise, lay his hand on an unresponsive brow, and question why he didn't feel more for the man when the man had never endeavored to feel more for him.

Dex smiled without joy, brandy a lingering burn. Maybe he'd threaten to marry the next suitable, no matter how repellant she or her family. Put Georgie to the test. A dare like none he'd placed before her. A true wager.

Her heart for his soul.

What would she do if he asked another woman to marry him while knowing he wanted *her*?

What would she do?

Nothing was a strong possibility.

He huddled into his coat, not his best, it had gone with Georgie, but good enough to keep out the worst of the foul weather.

He didn't want her gratitude or her compliance. He didn't want her to come to him because she'd decided she might like to be a duchess, a title he gave two figs about himself. Or because she was curious about what he could show her about the physical side of life, which from her stunned expression after he'd kissed her, was likely a lot.

He wanted her to come to him because she *trusted* him in the way she once had. Like a close friend she also happened to be frantically in love with.

The truth was, he wanted her to bet on him even if she believed she shouldn't.

## CHAPTER 7

The package arrived on Christmas Eve.

A simple white box wrapped with twine, no note accompanying it. With butterflies erupting in her belly, Georgie took the parcel to her chamber and laid it on the bed, staring at it in pained silence before wrapping the end of the string around her thumb and giving it a hesitant tug. Inside was a hooded cape the color of the lapis stone she'd nearly worn to dullness from her fretting caresses. Trimmed in fox fur and gold cord, the cape was more lavish than any she'd ever owned. More lavish than she needed. An intimate gift meant to send Dex's jarring avowal like a dart straight into the fleshy center of her heart.

*Make a list of how I should touch you, and I'll eagerly strike each off...*

Georgie pursed her lips and nudged the package closer. In the folds of tissue surrounding the cloak, she'd seen a flash of color. She lifted the beetle fossil from the box, brought it to her breast, and closed her eyes in anguish. Amusement. Fondness.

Blast him, the mischievous cad.

And a thief, she concluded, laughing until her stomach hurt. Because the fossil wasn't being returned to a German museum. Along with her lapis stone, she'd never relinquish it.

*Dexter Munro, what am I going to do with you?*

"You're going to find him a duchess, that's what," she answered, blinking the hearthfire into view. A mere hour from now, Edward Mullen, Viscount Lindley, and his family were arriving for a dinner party to introduce his daughter, Letitia, to the heir to the Duke of Markham. Lovely, lively, wholly appropriate Letitia. Handsome, clever, wholly available Dex.

They would make a gorgeous couple, have gorgeous children.

Live a gorgeous life.

The only wrinkle in the plan being he'd told her he wanted *her*. Georgie. His childhood friend. The scrap of a girl who'd tripped along behind him on a thousand artless adventures, hanging on his every word, recording his every move until she knew him better than she knew herself. In the end, she'd married out of necessity, like Dex was set to do. She'd survived her heart being smashed to bits. In any case, he couldn't possibly feel for her what she'd once felt for him; he would survive her gentle rebuff. The love she'd felt then could only belong to an impressionable girl, someone able to give entirely without knowledge about how vile relationships could be. Under the guise of matrimony, how much one had to lose.

How one could be hurt, damaged, changed.

*You're bitter,* Georgiana comprehended with a pulse of astonishment that had her slumping to the bed. *You're letting that horse's arse win.* She flopped to her back, arms outstretched, the fossil still clutched tightly in her fist. The ceiling had a tiny spider crack she traced with her eyes to the dark corner of the room. Her fury was fierce and precipitous, cleansing as well as harrowing. Three years after his demise, Arthur still had his fingers circling her wrist and was squeezing as she dropped to her knees. She flexed her hand, almost able to feel the pressure.

Dex's passionate response, lips sliding along her neck, warm breath stealing into her ear, returned to her on a wave of regret and yearning. He'd told her while they organized his fossils: *experience in every aspect of life lies in the details, and I love details.*

Georgiana palmed her quivering stomach and swallowed deeply.

What if, when she fantasized about lovemaking, images of Dex seized her mind instead of images of Arthur? Not the man of her dreams but the *real* man.

The resolution was easy.

Dex was a passionate man, and he, for his own reasons, wanted her.

She was passionate, she hoped, and she wanted him.

She could give him what he wanted, one night to satisfy *both* their needs. One night to wash away Arthur and her unhappy marriage for good. One night to show Dex she was a dream he'd created in his mind to ease the loneliness of being back in Derbyshire, the heartache of watching his father die. She was merely a woman he'd once known well, no more, no less. They could come together with no business arrangement attached, no contracts, no ticking clock, no weight of a hundred tenants on their shoulders. Simple want and desire allowed out of a cage, if those things were ever simple.

Passion for passion's sake.

Then he would be free to marry without worry he'd left anyone behind, and she would be free to never marry again.

For a potentially life-changing event, this dinner party wasn't any better than the last.

The lady was lovely. Excellent teeth and nice hair. Lavinia, Dex silently asked and sent a frowning glance into his wineglass. Lydia? Not that he could address her this casually even if they were appraising each other like horses at auction. He wouldn't be surprised if Viscount Lindley asked to see his molars. Dex threaded his fingers through his hair and gave the strands an exasperated tug. *Lord,* he was surviving on little sleep and too many damn questions he couldn't answer. Dex thought of his father rapidly failing in his massive tester bed at Markham Manor and realized the solution to his Twelfth Night promise did not reside in Georgie's leased dining room.

Unless you counted Georgie, and Dex didn't think he could.

She seemed anxious for this match to take.

The veranda door opened, and he stumbled back into the shadows, a rough smack against chilled stone.

"Dexter Reed Munro, you'd better come out right now!" Georgie said in an angry hiss.

Dex finished his wine, placing the glass on the ledge at his side. When Georgie stalked past him, he slipped his arm around her waist and tugged her into the darkened alcove. "Don't scream," he said in her ear, his body moving in to protect her from the fierce wind. "It's me."

Her breath caught, her arms clenching. "I'm going to murder you." She tipped her head, gazing at him from a circle of fox fur and gold trim. "A disappearing marquess is not reassuring, Dex. She'll think you don't want her."

"I don't."

Her curse was one he was surprised she knew.

"You're wearing the cape," he mumbled like a man waking from a dream. His world dissolved into shades of blue and silver, a winter wonderland. "This was the real Christmas present, a little early. The stone was an impulsive gesture."

Her mouth kicked, just the one side, so delightful a response his knees weakened.

"I don't want her," he echoed on a rushed breath, knowing he might as well be honest since Georgie was already mad about the entire evening. "I'm sorry. I know I must let my father know by Twelfth Night, and I'm running out of time, but Lydia wasn't the one for me."

"Letitia." With a sigh, she let her head fall against the stone, her eyes drifting closed. Her breath fogged the air, tepid gusts melting over his skin. "I told them you received a note about your father and had to rush home. Apologies were made, ones befitting a duke."

"It seems I'm not ready for polite society. Better with a pickax and a pile of rocks, as you said. Beneath the titles, there lies a humble geologist, though no one wants to believe it."

"I don't think I can help you with this," she whispered and lowered her gaze. "Your search for a duchess."

"Because I'm making it difficult?"

She paused for so long his ears started to sting from the cold. He had to get them inside before they froze to death.

"I would call it a conflict of interest," she finally murmured.

Blowing out a dumbfounded breath, Dex grabbed Georgie's hand and tugged her behind him through the slush, back into the house and into the first vacant room, which happened to be a cramped linen closet. Pushing her inside, he closed the door and leaned against it, darkness swallowing them. "We're not leaving this cupboard until you explain your comment."

"You said you wanted me." He heard her swallow, throat clicking. She exhaled softly, licked her lips if he wasn't mistaken. "The other day, by the carriage."

Like he didn't remember slicing a vein and bleeding in front of her?

He walked forward, bumping her back into the shelves. Grasping her hips, he drew her against his body, where it was *very* apparent he wanted her. A flash decision, he resolved to quit hiding the way he felt about her. He only had pride to lose, which wasn't much when compared to losing her. "I remember. I did. I *do*."

She gasped at the blatant feel of him, arching her back, a languid abrasion which made everything worse. "I can't think when you're touching me like this."

"And your point is...?" His hands curled around her waist as he pulled her deeper into the curve of his body. She wiggled with a staccato sound of pleasure, silky softness settling against his pulsing hardness. Regrettably, he was fast losing his focus. *Take her*, his body shouted while his mind grappled with more sensible options. "Hold a sec. I've forgotten my question."

"Oh bloody fine, Dex," she whispered, bounced up on her toes and slanted her lips over his.

They staggered into each other, seeking, awkward, off-balance. Then he lifted his hands to cradle her head, tipped his and...suddenly it was perfect. She moaned when they found the fit, and he drew the rushing cry into his mouth, because even ten seconds out, he'd never experienced a kiss like it. Hand sliding to the back of her neck, he bent over her, deepening the exchange, his tongue circling, mating, engaging. His other arm went low, where he lifted her from her slippers and against him. Her body strained, seeking. Closeness, closure. The scent of lavender and starched linen and Georgie wove a silken web around his awareness until he felt unattached, floating in space.

She shoved his chest, pushing him away from her and into the door. "A deal, Dex," she said, her breathlessness pleasing him to no end. "A pact. We make it here, agreed upon...by both parties."

He dropped his hands to her shoulders, slid them down her arms. Linking their fingers, he pulled her into him, whispered against her lips, "Do I need my solicitor for this negotiation?"

She fell into the kiss for a long, hypnotic instant, then wrenched her head to the side, sending his lips trailing along her cheek. "Dex, stop," she gasped. "Fight fairly for once."

He cursed beneath his breath and released her so abruptly he stumbled into a stack of folded towels, sending them scattering to the floor. His vision had adapted to the darkness, and she flooded into view, a curvaceous, irresistible shape eclipsed in shades of violet and gray. "Apologies. It's the wine." He loosened his cravat with a jerking pull, his breath flowing free in an aggravated gust. "Or my intense attraction to you. Or my loneliness." He slipped the length of silk from his neck and wadded it in a ball in his fist. "Take your pick."

"Or your need to win. Can I choose that option?"

His head came up, gaze finding her obscured one across the short distance. "Are we going to eradicate our desire with an argument? An age-old trick. Well done."

Her lips pressed, released. "I want to control for once. I lead, *you* follow. I deserve it after a lifetime spent shadowing you."

He shoved his cravat in her hand. "Tie my wrists to the bedpost, and I'll let you control everything."

Her head dropped, her fingers clenching around the silken square.

Then she asked the most unexpected question of his life, "Could you get loose?"

Astuteness or insight born from sympathy, *something*, saved him from approaching Georgie in the wrong way in that cracker box of a closet on a blustery Christmas Eve. Too forcefully, too selfishly, as most men would have with their cocks hard enough to bust buttons, fierce desire and greed racing through their bodies. He took a mental step back, examining the details he'd gathered about her. "Not if you didn't want me to, I couldn't. I wouldn't."

"I won't marry again," she murmured, the words so low he had to strain to hear them. "It's too late for me, that life."

His heart pitched in his chest, a deep, winded dive. He struggled to imagine what her declaration meant when he wanted more, and she knew it. He was, in turn, seduced and wounded. "Is that the deal? You gain experience. I teach. We part as friends when you return to London?"

Her hand settled over his thumping heart. "It's much more. I missed you dreadfully when you weren't a part of my life. Spending even this short amount of time with you here, at home, in Derbyshire....it's been wonderful. My first proper Christmas in years. I want your friendship. Forever, I want it. But I want this, too. I want *you*. I always have. I desire you as I desire no one." She halted his move to gather her close at her impassioned avowal, her fingers splaying over his chest. "Let me say this while I have the courage. So you understand."

"Georgie," he whispered, a plea, because he was falling swiftly in dire love with her—and he worried what she told him would further connect them in a way he'd be unable to break despite any promise he might make.

"When I said Arthur was cruel, I mean…" Her arm trembled, but she didn't release her hold on him. "When I close my eyes and imagine making love, I see nightmarish images instead of erotic ones. I want you to help me wipe those away. Replace ugly with beautiful. In turn, I want you to see what we share, you can find with another. You've already shared with another. This night will release us in different ways. Burdens of the past removed."

His teeth clenched in frustration, but he reigned the emotion in. "I'm trying very hard not to be insulted by this discussion, while the disreputable part of me is amenable to anything allowing me to tear your clothes off."

She issued a ghost of a laugh, and he imagined her cheeks heating to a seductive, rosy glow. "It's easier for a man. Not for me. Not when you're the only one I've ever wanted."

His breath and the last of his resistance left him. She was going to break his heart, be his downfall; this was clear. Might as well get on with it.

Leaning resignedly against the door, he brought her hand to his lips, pressing a rough kiss to the inside of her wrist. "I haven't been with leagues of women, Georgie. Enough, I suppose. But not so many that touching you will be anything but devastatingly momentous. An event which will leave me in tatters."

"Is that a yes?" she asked, the hand holding his cravat sliding to cradle his jaw, the sleek brush of silk against his skin making him shudder.

He nodded and lowered his lips to hers, allowing himself to believe he could change her mind about everything.

## CHAPTER 8

*G*eorgiana pulled him into a frenzied kiss at the bottom of the staircase, where they deposited his coat on the third step. Another against the morning room door, where her cape was left in a puddle on the floor. The last in the hallway outside her bedchamber, where she concluded the unfastening of his waistcoat, and he began fumbling with her bodice strings. A trip from the linen closet to her bed, usually taking three minutes, took ten and left her without thought or plan, her skin, every last inch, sensitized as if she'd rubbed a razor across it.

"Christ," he said against her lips, his breath churning as if he'd run a race, his fingers trembling where they cupped her jaw. "Which door is yours?"

She wrapped his cravat around his wrist, turned, and tugged him into her bedchamber.

He kicked the door closed, backed her against it, his lips falling to the nape of her neck. He bit gently, and she couldn't repress her moan. "You're sure, no servants? My coat, your cape…"

"Only three employed. It's a small manor. They return to the village each night. Widows do not require companions." She slipped his waistcoat from his arms and dropped it to the rug. "We're alone. *Completely*. Any noise you might like to make—"

He laughed, lifting her off her feet, walked two steps toward the bed, paused, his eyes changing, darkening. With one arm, he brought her down his body, an abrasive slide that had her knees threatening to weaken and leave her in a puddle at his feet. A spear of moonlight splashed across him, throwing his features into a tantalizing mix of shadow and light.

"What's that look, Dex?" Dear God, had he changed his mind?

He gazed at her, his collar twisted, the top two bone buttons of his shirt undone, the crisp linen parting to reveal a tantalizing smatter of dark hair. His eyes were the pale green of a lily pad, brimming with wonder when they met hers. Delighted and disheveled, he looked charmingly undone. "I've never…" He sighed, flexed his shoulders up and back. "Laughing, this lightness of spirit. It's never been fun. Not like this. I'm unprepared." He scrubbed his cheeks to hide their flooding with color. "Bloody hell, I think I'm nervous."

Her own delight was a wild beast charging through her body, dragging her heart away from her. "That makes two of us." She made quick work of releasing the remaining buttons and sent his shirt to the floor. "But I plan to work through it."

They disrobed with taunting kisses, whispered words of admiration and pleasure, learning each other's bodies through layers of wool, cotton, and muslin, then with no barriers at all. He was perfection, she decided, her gaze wandering from his narrow feet to his lean hips, flat stomach rippling with muscle, chest with a gorgeous sprinkling of hair, his entire body sculpted by his work. His career, his passion. She smiled. Maybe she could be his passion for at least one night.

"Do I amuse?" He curved his hand around her breast, cupping gently, his thumb brushing her nipple, circling, while his gaze held hers. Shifting, he blew a moist breath over the pointed tip, the pulse of visceral need catching her by surprise, darting like an arrow between her thighs. How clever, how wonderful.

Sighing deeply, she palmed his cheeks and brought his mouth closer, lifting her body, begging without words. *Touch me.*

"This?" he asked, his lips hovering deviously before he opened his mouth and sucked the bud inside.

"*Dex...*" She sagged, but he held her up, walked her back, all the while teasing her nipple into submission with his tongue, the edge of his teeth, fondling, encircling. He moved them to the bed, then startled her by turning to sit and bringing her atop him, positioning her bent legs on either side of his hips in a delicious straddle.

She sank onto his lap, his rigid length trapped between her thigh and his belly. "I've never...like this..." Dropping her head to his shoulder, she gasped as he nibbled on a sensitive spot below her ear. In return, she dug her teeth into his skin, the taste of him flowing into her mouth, a richness of feeling out the soles of her feet, absolute domination. His answering groan, hand tangling in her hair and drawing her mouth to his, told her everything she needed to know about how roughly he wanted to play.

About how fearless *she* could be.

Gathering her courage, she asked for more, felt his low laughter hit her cheek. "Impetuous Georgie." But he complied, his hand traveling over her breast, hip, thigh. When he came to the moist folds of her sex, he lingered, stroking and taunting, his mouth covering hers. After a breathless moment, he broke the kiss to slide his lips along her jaw, draw her earlobe between his teeth and suck, hard.

Her legs fell open, her hips pushing helplessly against his hand. Muscles in her thighs and arms clenching, she murmured meaningless words into the curve of his neck, damp strands of his hair sticking to her cheek. His skin had caught fire beneath her, burning. Finally, *yes, finally,* his finger eased inside, slowly, then back again. Patient, he allowed her to find the rhythm, determine the pace. She reached between their bodies, clumsy, indelicate, caught his hard length in her hand, circled, pressed, stroked. Learning the size and shape of him, sleek and solid and long. She'd never imagined touching Arthur in this manner, never considered it.

This was intuition alone driving her.

Hunger, avarice, enchantment.

Blind need, love, desire.

Another finger joined the first as he captured her lips beneath his, his movements on the brink of awkward, too, pleasing her because he was responding to her graceless touch, her body atop him, her breath in his ear, her teeth marking his skin.

The sensation started at the base of her spine. A sizzle, a surge that had her heart racing, her breath lodging in her throat. Dex leaned her back just enough to suck her nipple between his teeth. The stubble on his jaw scraped her, roughly, wonderfully, as he whispered something low and bewildered into her rounded flesh. The sounds she was making, helpless coos of delight, would have been embarrassing in any other arena, but here, in this dimly-lit chamber where Dex was turning her body inside out, it was natural.

She ran her thumb over the rounded head of his shaft, caught the drop of liquid, and felt his body jerk in response.

"So that's your game, is it? Two can play...that way." Groaning, he thumbed the inflamed bud between her legs, which needed only a second's care to toss her into a pool of decadent, haunting pleasure. The world rotated, listed, taking her with it in a dizzying spin as Dex rolled her to her back on the bed, his body flowing over hers, his weight pressing her deep into the mattress. Her vision went gray, her back arching as tremors raced through her, his fingers still claiming her, driving her, making her writhe in ecstasy.

Her cries mixed with his words of comfort and urgency.

Before she'd even landed, reclaimed her breath or reason or time, he was there, tenderly pushing inside her in gradual possession, inch by inch by inch. She quivered, the thrill of her body stretching to accommodate his sending another tiny shudder through her.

"You are," he murmured against her brow, her hair, her ear, "the most responsive...I never dreamed..." Changing the balance, he lifted her leg alongside his hip, perfecting the fit as they fell into a relentless, sinuous rhythm. Steady strokes, a hesitation, a gradual slide back.

A primal ballet.

She whimpered, clutched his shoulders, swept her hands down his back, nails digging, palms pressing. Teeth and lips, bowing, curving. Tongues tangling. Whispered pleas and tortured apologies, skin slick, quivering muscles, racing heartbeats. Again and again, until her only link to the world was where their bodies were joined.

"Tell me what you want," he breathed against her lips, his stroke constant, killing her with his control.

She grasped his hips, pulled him into her, fast, hard, not able to tell him what she needed, only able to *show* him. He dropped his head by her shoulder, sighed, moaned, agreed, his arms going around and under her, lifting her hips as he began to thrust, relentless, moving them up the bed.

Without interrupting his rhythm, he went to his elbow, lifted his head, a bead of sweat running down his jaw, the brutal pleasure on his face sending a fast throb through her core. She bowed into him, drawing him closer, welcomed lurid sensation into her forearms, her belly, the backs of her knees, the soles of her feet. Her body tightened. Alarmed, she looked into his eyes.

*Too much, this is too much.*

He smoothed her hair from her face, kissed her brow, murmured raggedly, "I'm here."

His words and the muted slap of their skin, his forceful yet delicate breach, the scent of their bodies mixing with each breath she took, seized every sensation and returned it on a rush unlike any she'd experienced, expanding her universe, then compressing it to a particle of sound, taste, touch. *I'm yours,* she thought, crying out against his shoulder as the vibrations overwhelmed her, circling from her core to flood her body.

An endless release, one he joined, brow to brow, nose to nose, cheek to cheek, gasping, shaking, clutching.

When she floated back to Earth, she couldn't speak, could only draw him into her, embracing his body and his seed, wondrously glad he hadn't left her. This, *this*, was unlike any experience of her life, unlike any dream, any fantasy. She realized how much she loved him, how incredible they were together, how it was going to destroy them both when she left.

She mentally stepped away and was lost, bereft.

*Oh, Georgie, what have you done?*

Dex rolled to his back and pulled her with him, tucking her against his chest, angling her knee over his belly, wrapping them in a moist, molten package. "I may never recover," he whispered, his voice breaking, throat raw. His lids fluttered, long lashes dusting his golden skin. "I hope not, anyway. My God, are you perfection. Are *we*."

She blinked back a salty sting, the lapis on the night table sitting in a puddle of moonlight, a steady glow in the darkened bedchamber. Dex's breath evened out, his fingers falling loose from where they'd been secured around her waist.

She could spend this time deciding what to do, what to say, how to go on with life, but right now, she'd accept the harmony and tenderness invading her soul. Breathe deeply of his scent and tangle her body with his.

Accept what he offered if only until morning.

~

He woke slowly, the silk sheet an invigorating caress, a subtle abrasion against sensitive skin. A gust through the window he'd cracked open after they made love before the hearth whispered over his body, the chill crisp and calming. A floral scent—lavender?—and woodsmoke permeated the room, the bedding they lay tangled in, her hair, a wild, flaxen mass covering her face and his. A slice of spring in the middle of winter.

He elbowed to a half-sit, stretched, yawned, depleted in the best of ways.

And Georgie...

Dust motes fluttered through the flickering rays of dawn to shimmer over her. She lay on her side, arm tucked beneath her cheek, chest rising and falling in a bottomless, exhausted tempo.

They had worn each other to the bone.

The first time in his life he'd utterly surrendered himself. And the last if, when she awoke, she got dressed and left him, as he feared she planned to do.

Lifting his fingers before his face, he inhaled their scent, lush and earthy. The memories of the night were razor-sharp, bringing with them arousal so robust, Dex was left with the choice to wake her for another round or walk it off. Drawing the sheet to her shoulders, he gave it a neat tuck and slipped from the bed, searched the room until he located his trousers in a wad under the chaise lounge along with one of her slippers. Good enough, he resolved and tugged them on, because he'd no idea where he'd tossed his drawers in the frenzy.

He prowled the room, gathering clothing, lighting candles, stoking the fire into a blaze that would quickly chase out the chill. He also looked for clues to solve the mystery of the Ice Countess, the Georgie he didn't know but feared.

*I was supposed to be her first,* he reasoned with irrational venom, dusting the heel of his hand over his heart, conflicted, jealous, guilt-ridden. What an utterly masculine bit of idiocy the statement was. Possessive to the extreme. He knew she wouldn't like it, although he couldn't help but feel it.

He'd *always* felt it.

Startled by his perplexing emotions, he paused at the window, staring into the snow-shrouded distance, the Derbyshire hills and valleys he loved almost as much as he loved her. "No one understood how to touch you," he whispered and trailed his finger through the mist his breath was painting on the pane. "How to make you come alive." This much about her he'd figured out. A soft approach with Georgie was vital. He'd relinquished control, let her hold the reins, drive his carriage. She'd been abused, her confidence shaken, her sense of self destroyed. At a time in life when one was discovering oneself, she'd been thrust into a relationship with a man old enough to be her father, a heartless man from the little she'd imparted, a man Dex would gladly kill if he stood before him.

She hadn't known herself fully until he'd taken the time to show her.

Dex hadn't known himself, either. Honestly, he hadn't.

Watching her sensuality flower and bloom had been nothing short of the most magical sexual experience of his life. Part of him had bloomed with her.

Glancing at the bedside table, he noticed the jewel beetle he'd stolen from a German museum sitting among other personal effects. The lapis, a hair clip, a crimson ribbon, an olive-green glass bottle. He wondered if this was all she'd have of him. A damned chunk of stone and a filched fossil. He sank to the window seat, his oath muttered against his closed fist so as not to wake her.

He was fit for no one. Georgie had ruined him, utter destruction.

He hoped she'd be happy when she realized this.

"Is foul language part of the seduction? I think I like it."

He snapped his head up, embarrassed and provoked. The sweet, teasing fire in her eyes only brought him closer to doom. His emotions were tender, his chest aching. He debated, then decided touching her right now would be a mistake and stayed where he was.

"Merry Christmas, Dex."

*Christmas.* He'd almost forgotten.

"I didn't separate from you the first time," he shocked himself by saying, thinking he'd love nothing more than to have a child with her, but if he admitted this, she'd run back to London like he'd lit a fire beneath her lovely bottom. "A risk for which I humbly apologize. I was overcome with—" He laughed, his temple knocking the window frame before he located her gaze again. "Hell, I couldn't think, I could barely breathe I was so taken with you, with us." He shrugged, scratched a nonexistent itch on his chest. "I have no words. I told you I wasn't charming, not by half. This impressive speech proves it."

Georgie tucked her bottom lip between her teeth in a move he grasped meant she was reasoning something out. He believed she wanted to laugh, which might not have gone over well. "Did I say I minded?" she finally whispered, sitting, letting the sheet plunge to her waist.

This was his first view of her in abundant light, and his pulse skipped, his mouth going dry. His childhood friend and the woman he loved melded into one. He fell hard, like a boulder over a cliff.

"I have five days until I return to London," she said after a strained silence, her gaze sweeping from his bare feet to his neck and back again—the heat of her regard turning him to ash.

At least she seemed as entranced with his body as he was with hers.

His heart skipped a beat, two, as his blood raced through his veins. But he didn't move, didn't blink. If she wasn't going to give him what he wanted—*forever*—he was going to make her construct the dwelling they were set to momentarily settle in and beg him to visit. "Five days for what?"

A long sigh left her with the rise and fall of her shoulders. "You're frustrated because I'm not yielding to your wishes for once. The girl tripping along behind you is all grown-up, Dex. She has her own needs and wants and, yes, *wishes* now."

"After last night, I'm well aware. Very grown-up, indeed." He produced a phony yawn when his stomach was twisting into knots. "We've gone over this in triplicate. I'm resigned, not frustrated. I adore your tenaciousness, except when it gets in the way of what I want. There, I've admitted it. I like to get my way."

"An impasse, because I do, too."

"Then, the farce continues."

Georgie plucked at the sheet, looking like she was considering snatching it to her neck if they were going to argue. "You make finding a duchess sound as appealing as tossing out the contents of a chamber pot."

"That about covers it."

Sliding off the bed, Georgie crossed to him, her naked body a glorious thing in the bracing, pearly light of dawn. She had a knowing luster in her eyes only a woman of proficiency can obtain. He'd given her this and now felt like prey being tracked by a more cunning animal.

"What can I do to wipe away your fierce glower?" she asked with the barest hint of a smile. Enough of one to send her dimples roaring to life, the ideal time for them to appear, damn her. "My Christmas present to you."

His gaze sharpened, his body tightening. "I don't know. What can you?"

Going to her knee, she gathered his cravat from the rug and

looking up at him, pulled it through her fingers. "How good are your knots, Dex?"

His breath left him in a rush. "You'd let me do this? Control you in this way?"

She wrapped the length of snowy-white silk around her fist, gave it a firm tug. "I trust you. You're my closest friend. Everything between us flows from that reality."

Slipping a hand beneath her elbow, Dex pulled her to her feet, his intent gentle but possessive as his mouth captured hers. Love was a dull blade carving him in two, but he could not, would not, admit it. Suffering to last a lifetime lay down that path.

Georgiana's arms went around his neck as he turned and pressed her to the wall. His cravat fluttered heedlessly to the floor. They didn't need it. He needed nothing but her.

"I'll take the five days," he whispered against her lips. "And your Christmas gift."

But he couldn't help but think as he lost himself in her—*and when it's over, I'll release you even if it kills me.*

# CHAPTER 9

Over the next five days, Georgiana glanced up from making notes in Dex's folio and caught him gazing at her with the same bookish expression he carried when he categorized fossils. And at other times, too. After they made love, across a candlelit dining table, walking the moors, the look was there, searching, probing when she'd told him exactly what she was thinking, why she had to return to London, why she didn't want to remarry.

Simple statements of fact when nothing was simple.

Opting to embrace cowardice, she'd revealed all except the critical fact that she loved him with every part of her being. If this deadly admission slipped free, he wouldn't let her leave when the time came, which it would in twenty-four hours.

Pushing aside the gloomy comprehension that had sneaked past pleasure, Georgiana lifted shakily to her elbow from her spot on the floor, where she and Dex had tumbled during a rather acrobatic session on the bed. "Are you injured? You managed to spin us around and take the brunt of the fall. It was awe-inspiring."

Dex yanked the tangled sheet off his face, revealing moss green irises. The more relaxed, the darker his eyes. Over the past week, this had proven to be a fascinating study. "I told you not to twist that way. You nearly snapped off an essential part of my anatomy."

She laughed and rolled to face him, her hand going to his bottom lip. It was plump and moist, battered from her attention. She'd had it caught between her teeth when they took their tumble. In retribution, he grasped her fingertip and sucked on it until her vision blurred.

"But you liked it," she gasped.

Releasing her, he shook his head, his gaze going to the ceiling. "You know I loved it. I made enough noise to wake the ghosts in this place. Don't try to catch me in your feminine trap, have me confessing what you do to me. Leave me with a slight crumb of dignity."

She propped her head on her hand, questioning how she was going to survive without him. His habits had become part of her routine, part of her joy in the day, pleasure *outside* the bedchamber. The way he folded his newspaper into a neat square and shoved it under his breakfast plate so he could read without handling; the way he paced while tossing a rock from hand to hand when he considered a vexing geological theory; the way his nose crinkled when he laughed; the way he rolled his sleeves into faultless folds on his forearms; the way he held her hand, lightly but forcefully, when they walked the heaths as if he feared she was preparing to run away from him; the way his pupils expanded a tick before he leaned in to kiss her.

Being exposed to such intimate details of a man's life had started to change the way she looked at relationships, and her belly quivered with this understanding. She feared she'd been teaching her young ladies the wrong things—

*No.* She frowned, not wrong. She'd been teaching without actual knowledge. Relationships *could* provide the opportunity for great passion. For love. Her gaze roved Dex's face. High cheekbones, strong jaw. Hair too long, lips too full. And his body, *God*, his gorgeous, athletic, magnificent body. Maybe more men than she'd anticipated were out there, seeking affection and understanding, vulnerable in a way she'd not imagined a man could be. Like many women were. She palmed her aching chest and swallowed hard.

How had she been so mistaken about life?

"I can feel your thoughts churning," he whispered when she believed he'd slipped to sleep, a feat he accomplished quicker than anyone she'd ever known. Turning on his side to face her, he mirrored her posture, head in hand, gaze drowsy but steady. "I'll pay a halfpenny for them but no more. That's my final offer."

"I think I've misled my apprentices," she blurted, then hoped she'd recover without admitting what she was feeling. Too much, too befuddled, too jumbled. And Dex would pounce on her confession like a starved lion.

A tiny dent flowed between his brows. Another fascinating thing she'd noticed, this worrying dink. "How so, Georgie girl?"

Her gaze roamed the rug with the tattered edge, the ceiling with the spider crack, the narrow slice of moonlight shooting through a grimy windowpane. The manor she'd leased wasn't in the best condition, but she loved it, was cozy and happy and satisfied.

But she feared her happiness was all due to Dex.

"Uh-huh." He tipped her chin until her gaze had nothing to do but return to him. "How so?"

His quiet way of listening had proven hazardous to her secrets, encouraging her to tell him everything about her disaster of a marriage, her resentment toward her father for putting her in such a position, her hopes for the Duchess Society. *Everything.*

Except for the *I-love-you* part.

"I didn't know it could be like this, I could be like this," she murmured. "I had such bitterness in my heart and my view that my marriage was representative when perhaps it was not, and now I've unintentionally provided erroneous guidance. Toxic guidance even. A veritable Ice Countess releasing venom on society. A bad example, when I never imagined I would be, tainting what I touch."

"I didn't know it could be like this, either. Therefore you're forgiven." His tone was impassive, hard to decipher. His lids drifted low like they did when he wanted to hide his feelings. "You're realizing what we have. But I can see from the firm set of your lovely jaw you're still set to make us pay for Arthur's mistakes. Me, especially, when I'd kick the man's arse from here to Piccadilly if he still took air. It's ludicrous the statutes you're imposing but my hands, as they were last night against these very bedposts, are tied."

A bitter gust raced in the open window and drifted across their skin, still moist from loving each other this eve. Twice, in relatively rapid succession. Georgiana shivered, Dex cursed. With a twist, he yanked the counterpane from the bed and tossed it none too gently over her.

She pulled her head out from beneath the coverlet, blew a strand of hair from her face. "What would you have me do, Dex?"

He snorted, his eyes when they met hers flashing with fury. Banked to the color of a fallen tree, a dozen shades of brown and black. His palm slapped the floor as he reared to a sit. "Really, Countess Winterbourne? Shall I go down on one knee *again*?"

"You haven't gone down on *any* knee, Dex. You've only suggested what I should do, in your opinion. Always in your opinion. When you know I'm confused. When you know I used to do anything you asked of me, which is part of the problem. You expect my compliance, demand it even. Come along, Georgie girl, and do what I request of you. Don't think about it because I've done the thinking for you!"

He stilled, considering what she'd said. It broke her heart, made her love him more. She'd never known another man who actually *listened*. "Had I asked for your hand all those years ago, would you have said yes?"

Her breath caught as they stared, unable to look away from each other. This was a dream she'd once wished for, prayed for. *Oh, if only...if only...* Beneath the counterpane, her hand tightened into a fist.

In the end, she nodded, the silent admission ripped from her.

"A most remarkable blunder." His oath was violent. "My hands are still shaking," he said and held them out so she could see them trembling. "Just so you know, I'd stalk right from this chamber to fully communicate my despondency if my legs would hold me."

"I'm not in any better shape to bring you back like I did last night." But his apology, offered on the sweeping staircase leading to her bedchamber, had been *delightful*.

He slumped against the bedpost, head hanging, throat flexing. "You're leaving tomorrow, Georgie. I know I agreed to this, but I'm starting to panic."

She licked her lips, crimping the counterpane's frilled seam between her fingers. "What if you came to visit me occasionally—"

"What about my wife? That silly duchess person." He made an inane gesture, an insult to his future spouse. "Do I bring her as well? Tell her not to worry as we're childhood friends-turned-lovers. Pay no mind, darling, everyone in the *ton* does it. Very progressive, this marriage. No fault of yours it's with the wrong woman."

Georgiana pressed the heel of her hand to her belly, forcing back the queasiness rippling through her. "Oh, God." She drew her knees up, dropped her cheek to them. "That won't work. I'll scratch her eyes out if I get within reach."

The silence thumped like a heartbeat between them. They'd done this before, waited out the hush until one of them broke. Usually her. She was finding Dex to be extremely hard of head and steady of mind. A log snapped in the hearth, a mantel clock counted off the seconds. The scent of lavender and sandalwood, smoldering birch and mating bodies, filtered in and gave her heart a hard twist.

"You're not really going to leave, are you?" he finally asked in a stark murmur.

She rolled her head to look at him just as he lifted his to look at her. His eyes were losing their acidity and sliding back to a pale, approachable hue. "I have an interview with the Earl of Nottenworth's daughter in four days. Camilla is beautiful and temperamental and practically abandoned by her family. Her father has gambled away the fortune. Her brother, Vincent, is an absolute bounder. She cannot enter the upcoming Season without support. She simply cannot."

A muscle in Dex's jaw flexed. "Your support."

"Mine and Hildy's." Her partner, Hildegard Templeton, had agreed to manage the Duchess Society while Georgiana traveled for the holiday but this was a temporary arrangement. Georgiana's temper sparked as Dex continued to stare as if his searing gaze would change her mind. They were naked, after all, and it had happened before.

"Why is your surveying so important, all those blessed fossils, every split of rock from here to India, when my work is not? Is it because I'm a woman? Please enlighten me, Dex. I'd love to hear why my career, unique though it may be, is not valuable to society when yours is."

His top lip canted, escalating her irritation. She'd no idea why her displeasure often made him smile. "I have an idea, Georgie girl."

"Oh," she whispered and dug her face into her knees. Dex's ideas were legendary. Legendary debacles. Like the time they'd spent the night in one of those limestone caves he cherished after misjudging the daylight and getting lost. It had been exciting, a remarkable adventure, even as she'd questioned if they'd make it home. It was one of her fondest memories of Anthony. Her brother had laughed as the darkness rushed in on them, fearless, the most daring man, aside from Dex, she'd ever known.

Dex took her hand, turned it palm up, and started drawing deliberate circles that caused her skin to heat, her body to burn. "Believe it or not, my responsibilities are luring me to London as well. A legal issue with a tenant on one of the Yorkshire estates requiring consultation with the family's solicitor. Also, there's a government committee I'm scheduled to discuss the Wales expedition with, details of the start date, funding, equipment, and such. I can do much via messenger, but not all. The correspondence back and forth regarding each is killing me."

She blinked, lifted her head. "Yorkshire estates. As in two?"

He drew up his leg, hooked his arm around it, and propped his chin on his wrist. She completed a comprehensive study from his unruly hair to his very masculine toes, unable to check the impulse. His skin, still damp, glistened in the firelight. His body was simply breathtaking, and her fingers itched to touch.

He sputtered out a laugh. "I'm supposed to talk to you while you look at me like *that*?"

Her cheeks flushed as she lifted her gaze to his. If he laughed again, she would punch him.

"Georgie, you've no idea the hardship this ducal title brings. More responsibility than funds allow for. I'm to be burdened with two residences in London, two estates in Yorkshire, Markham Manor you're acquainted with, plus a charming castle of sorts in Ireland to round out the bunch. Accountability for the village here, which you know I've been reviewing improvements for. I've only visited the Irish castle once and plan to take my charming bride there, conceivably for an entire summer as a research project on the Cliffs of Moher has been presented to me. The first Duke, a staunch Royalist, fled there after being expelled from the House of Lords in 1642. The home is haunted, the whole bit. And lovely, from my memory. Romantic." He sighed, his lids dipping low, his lashes a neat sweep against his skin. "I'd hoped to have her, the duchess, that is, travel with me to Wales for an upcoming expedition, too. Not many wives accompany their husbands on these excursions, that's true, but for the right woman, the absolutely *perfect* one, which is what I'm tasked with finding, it could be advantageous for both parties. It could be, dare I dream, *fun*."

Georgiana squinted as he pressed his lips together to hold back his laughter. He was tempting her with what she sought to reject. Dangling all that appealed before her, like *he* appealed, every last bit of him. His flat tummy, his chest covered in what she'd determined to be the ideal amount of hair, his wickedly charming smile, those eyes. *Oh, she did love his eyes.* His wit, his sly humor, his intelligence. Hair no man in London could claim, in shades of ginger and gold. "You are a scoundrel," she groused.

He shrugged, scratched his chin with his thumb. "I propose we table this discussion until Twelfth Night because I want to triumph, which is, at present, not occurring. Six days to ponder our noteworthy circumstances and what each of us wants from the other with two hundred miles of terrain separating us. A fair distance, that."

Her mind whirled, her thoughts dizzying. This was another roundabout proposal—the most enticing one yet. Lots of pull without all the push. "Your father?"

"His condition has improved enough that I can leave for a few days, and these issues aren't going to disappear because I wish like bloody hell they would. And I can't help him, much as I find I'd like to.

I'm doing no good pacing his bedchamber an hour each day and talking to the walls."

"What of your promise?"

"I plan to fulfill my promise." He leaned to tuck a strand of hair behind her ear. Her breath left her in a soft sigh Dex wouldn't miss. He looked away, his jaw clenching. "In London, it seems."

"What I'm hearing is you expect I'll miss you so much I go blind."

His laugh was clipped but exuberant, surprising them both. "I'm not sharing the details of my plan, darling. What kind of strategy is that?" He leaned even closer, his lips skimming hers. More the fool, she didn't move away. "Perhaps I'll roam the cobbled city streets searching for the perfect duchess. Since your beloved society has not provided able assistance."

She made a sound, either a groan or a sigh, and his pupils expanded, flooding those gorgeous eyes. Then he was kissing her, hand tangling in her hair and drawing her against him, bare skin melding as they reached and strained. Gasping breaths and desperate appeals. Sizzling contact with a bite, nothing sweet about it.

Before the world dissolved into hazy hues, she shoved him back. He'd been lowering her to the rug, and she knew where the party went from there. "Six days."

His lips parted as he blinked. "What?"

Poor man, she thought, kissing himself senseless. "Six days. And we meet on neutral territory."

He paused, considered, nodded. "January 5. The British Museum. Natural history room. One o'clock."

Georgiana rolled her eyes. Only a man of science found a museum romantic. "They only conduct personal tours, Dex. You have to have connections, be a member. I tried once before to gain entry and was denied."

His answering grin was hypnotic. "Georgie, half the rocks in the place are mine. I can gain entry. I'll send my carriage for you, let's make it noon."

He believed he had her. Wrapped nice and tight, when this was the first time she'd been free. Having a delicious love affair, no husband in sight, her own means of income, however trivial. *Free*. That was quite something to consider giving up. Vexing, arrogant male. "I'll get myself to the museum at one o'clock without your assistance, thank you. I have transport, pitiful state the carriage is in, but it's mine."

Dex pulled her into his arms and rolled her to her back, his laughter echoing off the crack in the ceiling and smooth as silk, slipping right through it. "Not going to give an inch, are you, Georgie girl?"

She brought his lips to hers, whispered against them, "Darling, what kind of strategy would that be if I did?"

# CHAPTER 10

*D*ex missed her enough to go blind.

He'd come to London the day after Georgie and done some very embarrassing things since then. Ridden by her townhouse twice, visited her favorite bookstore and a tea shop on Strand she frequented. Searched the gossip sheets for a mention of the Ice Countess, popped in White's, which he loathed, perusing the betting book in the event she was listed. Even made an appearance at an excruciating musicale in the hopes she'd be in attendance. These endeavors doing nothing but creating a heightened state of unease—because the woman hadn't said no, but hadn't, in any manner, said *yes*.

Then, there were the gifts. Delivered to Georgie's residence like clockwork.

Somehow, he couldn't help himself.

He'd never had anyone to court or shower with, well, *love*. Dogged, when he finally put his mind to the process of courting. And starry-eyed, which was an absolute surprise. A hard knock to his plan to stay hidden all this gallivanting around, shopping for fripperies, and peeping from carriage windows. The damned broadsheets had made mention of his attending the musicale and maybe even the bookstore. Marked as looking for a duchess, which was right in a broad sense.

Now Georgie knew he was in London, but so did all the overeager mothers.

He was flooded with calling cards, invitations, requests for tea—but only silence from his girl.

He tossed his quill to the desk and sent ink splattering across his ledgers. Chauncey thought it daft, but Dex had chosen to rent rooms on St. James rather than stay in the Mayfair residence or the cottage in Richmond Park, both so much his father's spaces Dex couldn't embrace them, even if he'd been managing every aspect of their survival for years. For a few more days, conceivably for the last time, he wanted to sleep on a squeaky bed, conduct his research at a desk nicked from time, pace warped planks, and dispassionately record life from a grimy windowpane. Though his current view offered little beauty. No rolling hills, no verdant swathes of woodland stretching to the horizon. No scent of charred wood or turned earth or frost-coated pine needles.

His dilemma? He missed Derbyshire almost as much as he missed Georgie.

In a way, they'd become one in his mind, in his heart.

He'd walked the moors with her, the forbidding wind stealing across the desolate expanse capturing their breath and pinkening her cheeks. Two loves of his life intrinsically linked. It rose above the physical what he felt for her, above the emotional, as it did for the untamed land in the north.

So layered, his feelings, a mere man had no hope of explaining them.

He only knew it *was*.

He pressed his hand to his heart, holding back the familiar ache. She didn't *need* him. Her efforts in the past month had been her way of telling him this. Her marriage to Arthur had wrought significant damage, damage running soul-deep. It was up to Georgie to decide if the love of a geologist posing as a gentleman was sufficient to heal her wounds.

He could do no more, or not much, Dex determined, as he grabbed his hat and coat and rang for his carriage. It was time to shop for today's gift. The last, because tomorrow was Twelfth Night.

Tomorrow, he would find out if Georgie was any readier to be a duchess than he was to be a duke.

～

Georgie missed him enough to go blind.

And for the past three days, he'd made every effort to increase her loneliness.

She stared at the parcel resting on the escritoire between a brass hair clip and Lady Anton's creased calling card. The package was as attractive as the others Dex had sent, a rose-pink ribbon drawn about brown paper and sealed with crimson and gold wax.

The last gift, as their meeting at the museum was taking place tomorrow.

In nineteen hours, to be exact.

Georgiana lifted her gaze to the gilded mirror on the wall, bringing the wrapped box to her breast. She felt different. Did she look it? Was she forever changed? She pinched her cheek, swept her hand down her throat, which only brought to mind the memory of Dex's teeth catching the tender skin beneath her ear and sucking as she moaned, craved, *begged*.

Raw yearning flooded her, weakening her knees until she had to brace a hand on the desk to steady herself.

Her need was potent.

When she'd never needed a man, never allowed herself the option. Never been presented the option. And now, for the first time, it had happened. When she was liberated. The word rang through her mind like the din of a church's bell.

Liberated from *what* exactly, her heart asked?

Since leaving Derbyshire, she'd been free of Dex's wicked smile, tender touch, knowing glances. His intelligence, his humor, his fiery temper. His long leg thrown over hers in the shelter of their bed. His hot breath washing across her skin as he thrust inside her.

In the mirror, she watched her cheeks color in a way no amount of pinching brought.

She was enslaved, gladly welcoming the chains of love circling her. *I need him.* Above all else, above love, above reason, need was the critical piece.

The necessary piece, vital.

She only had to find the courage to tell him.

The click of the door startled her, and the box tumbled from her hand.

Lady Hildegard Templeton paused in the sitting room entrance, glanced at the pretty parcel lying on the faded Axminster rug, letting a furtive smile spill free. Aside from Dex, Hildy was Georgiana's favorite person in the world, her dearest friend, her mentor of sorts. Daughter to an earl, at an incredibly young age, Hildy had found the fearlessness to rise above what society expected of a woman of her station. Georgiana greatly admired her. Hildy had studied alongside her brother's tutors, eventually surpassing what they could teach her. She raced her phaeton through Hyde Park while wordlessly daring any man she met to tumble, such was her beauty and uniqueness. Called a bluestocking to her face and worse behind closed salon doors, she'd stunned the *ton* by refusing to marry, believing one wedded for love, an idea society mocked. Her mission with the Duchess Society was to ensure other women had the support to choose as she had or be educated regarding the business of matrimony if they did not.

Hildy closed the door and cocked a slim hip against it. "Another one? My, your darling duke is persistent."

Georgiana went to her knee to retrieve the package. "The marquess is not my darling anything, Hildy." Which might not be true after tomorrow. Her hand shook to imagine it.

"He's your darling anything should you want him." Hildy laughed as she crossed the room, the amused echo as pleasing as her visage. Even with her scandalous reputation, Hildy had admirers, yet she said none made her heart sing. Ditchdigger or viscount, she cared nothing about a title and refused to settle for less than a warbling heart.

Unlike Georgiana five short weeks ago, Hildy didn't expect love to strike, but she believed it *could*.

Georgiana fiddled with the ribbon, twisting it around her finger as Hildy's shadow waterfalled over her. She glanced up, encountered her friend's knowing smile, dimples, dear heaven, pinging *both* cheeks. It was no wonder men collapsed at Hildy's feet.

"Open it, the suspense is stealing my breath," Hildy said and offered her hand.

Georgiana took it, levering to a stand.

"Can't be chocolates. That was yesterday." Hildy released her satin chin strap and ripped the plaid bonnet from her head. "The day before was the fox fur muff to match your cape. A practical *and* sentimental choice. Scented soap, a leather-bound volume of poetry you clasped to your chest and mooned over all morning. An outrageously extravagant brooch you've worn since. What am I forgetting?"

Georgiana threw Hildy a chilling glance and yanked on the package's ribbon until it loosened and fell into her hand. "I don't know why you're enjoying this so much." If her friend realized how personal each gift truly was—the soap honeysuckle, her favorite scent; the brooch meant to replace one she'd lost on the moors years ago; the book of poems by Keats, whom she treasured without question; the tea, a gift Hildy had forgotten to mention, from her favorite shop—Hildy would force Georgiana into her carriage and deposit her on Dex's doorstep on St. James this very minute.

Astonishingly, Hildy had shown herself to be a romantic.

"I'm enjoying this because you're happy, maybe for the first time. Those nasty shadows under your eyes departed, your smile genuine. You've been humming, do you know that? Humming! I'll welcome any man as a friend who can bring such joy. Plus, what a boon for the society if we snag an actual duke! The Duchess Society's name will be validated." Hildy took the gift from Georgiana and removed the paper, raised a brow in challenge. "Shall we open the last, Georgie?"

"Oh, I shouldn't have mentioned the nickname." Georgiana shifted from one slippered foot to the other and tangled her fingers in her

# THE ICE DUCHESS

skirt. "It's silly, something from the past, something Lord Munro started calling me when I was just out of leading strings. It's childish."

"No," Hildy said in all seriousness, "it perfectly suits. He knows you well, I'm thinking."

Georgiana bumped her bottom to the desk with a sigh of exasperation, dropping her face to her hands. "That's what I'm afraid of, what I want more than life. I'm a mess, an absolute snarl."

Hildy stepped in, pulled her close. "It's acceptable, even recommended in this case, to love him. You can still be the capable woman you want to be. With the right man, I believe it's possible. In fact, I think the society will be the better for it. Two vastly different marital experiences to use as a guide for our young ladies. What understanding you'll have." Hildy hugged her, a gesture that sent a torrent of affection rushing through Georgiana. "Allow yourself to love him if this is where your heart wants to go. He's proven himself to be loyal and incredibly steadfast."

"I should have sent him a note thanking him for the gifts." She chewed on her bottom lip, knocked the toes of her slippers together. "I've made him wait, worry when he doesn't know I want to say yes."

Hildy straightened, her breath streaking out in surprise. "He's asked then?"

Georgiana took the box from Hildy's hand, smiled softly. "In lots of ways."

"Well..." Hildy's fingers went to the desk and did a nervy tap.

The last gift was the most personal.

Georgiana unfolded the map, seeing Dex had made small checkmarks next to the places he wanted to take her. Some for his geological work, some for pleasure. *The world can be ours*, he'd whispered in the hushed Derbyshire twilight, his arms tight about her. Paris, Munich, Cardiff, Edinburgh, Florence. With her finger, she traced the Arno river and remembered Dex telling her how much he loved Tuscany. There was an exquisite villa near the *Ponte alle Grazie* he'd stayed in once, and he was desperate to return.

With her.

"Rather disappointing," Hildy murmured, "when he was doing so well with the gifts. But for a man of science, he's done an excellent job overall."

Georgiana brought the map to her lips, dropped her head, and sighed against it.

"Oh." Hildy bumped Georgiana's shoulder and giggled low in her throat. "You like it. A dingy, old map, but you like it. Odd, but certainly wonderful he didn't disappoint, that you understand the significance."

"I love it." *I love him. I want him. I* need *him.*

"A map as welcome as a diamond?" Hildy dusted her hands together as a blinding smile lit her face. "It's decided, you're perfect for each other. You're to love an academic. And God knows, someone should."

"He wants to give me the world, Hildy." She glanced again at the map while she negotiated with her heart. "And you know what? I think I'll take it."

## CHAPTER 11

*A promise fulfilled on Twelfth Night...*

Dex shoved his hands in his greatcoat pockets and shivered. The day was frigid, the sky reconciled between wretched and ghastly, icy splinters sneaking beneath the brim of his beaver hat to strike his cheek. As he crossed Great Russell Street, his heart, like the sky, was leaden, his chest taut, making breath a rare commodity. He was barging inside the first public house he encountered, no matter how appalling, and not coming out for days. He was going to drown himself in the finest spirits the district of Bloomsbury had to offer—and then he was going to start on the worst. Maybe he'd unleash his temper, use his fists to alleviate his misery. It'd been years since he'd used them in this manner, but it likely wouldn't be the last.

Georgie hadn't shown.

He'd waited in the damned natural history bay for one hour, his donated rocks mocking him, then stalked from room to room should she have gotten lost amidst the group of Oxford professors who'd been wandering the halls since morning. Had he confused the time? Done something to offend her? That blasted map, he thought and gave the bridge of his nose a hard pinch.

The least traditionally romantic gift of all he'd given, but the most personal.

Had she hated it? Not grasped it's meaning? He was asking her to stay with him, to travel with him, to *be* with him.

Offering his heart and all that went with it.

He didn't know how to impress a woman. He'd never known.

Dread cut a wide path through him. It was simple: Georgie wasn't going to allow herself to love him again.

In a burst of confidence, he'd even sent a missive to his father. The Duke of Markham had always loved Georgie. He'd be pleased to know Dex did, too.

When all Dex had done was curse himself.

He bumped into a man exiting a bootmaker's shop and snarled a rude rejoinder when he was utterly at fault. She didn't love him; this was obvious. Not enough, in any case. Didn't want to be his duchess, which he understood. Who truly desired that ridiculous title and the mess that went with it? But if Georgie loved him, the future Duke of Markham, if she needed him as he needed *her*, the duchess piece was, unfortunately, part of his package.

The velvet box in his waistcoat pocket sizzled and stung, a woeful little weight reminding him of his idiocy. He should have asked her to marry him years ago, after their impetuous kiss. When she'd had stars in her eyes and no memory of an earl who'd married her and made her life miserable. She'd admitted she would have said yes. They'd been young, but his heart hadn't shifted since then. Not one tick. Now, she had more pressing issues to be concerned with. Bigger dreams. Her society, a group spoken about in apprehensive tones by the inhabitants of White's. Viscount Reading's cheeks had paled when he mentioned his betrothed was meeting with Georgiana the following week to discuss how best to settle their marital contract. The woman he loved had the *ton* by the short hairs, and Dex could almost, *almost* laugh about that.

When he got over feeling like he wanted to cry instead.

Halting in front of St. George's, he climbed the church steps and let the crowd pass, unsure what to do next. Perched against a marble column that felt like a block of ice, he'd worked himself into a sufficient despondency when he heard someone shouting his name.

He looked up, dizzily, blood draining from his head to pool at his feet.

Georgie was hanging half out of a hackney window as it bounced down the street and into the curb, her bonnet, if she'd had one, long gone, her chignon destroyed by the wind and sleet. Before the driver got off his box, Dex was there, ripping open the carriage door and pulling her into his arms right on the sidewalk while a crowd of pedestrians funneled past.

"Oh, Dex, I'm sorry." Her face was tear-streaked, her nose as red as the holly berries he'd sprinkled along a Derbyshire hallway so she could find him. "My carriage hit ice and lost a wheel as they were bringing it around this morning. I had to locate other transport after making sure my coachman wasn't injured and—"

His gloved hands rose to frame her chilled cheeks. "Georgie girl, hush. I'm here. It's okay."

She broke down then, absolutely distraught. Agonized pleas he couldn't make out mixed with sobs and hiccups. Worry about his finding his duchess at a musicale or on the street in front of a millinery.

Her adorable hysteria dropped him deeper in the pit of love.

Taking her by the arm, he guided her up the steps and into St. George's while murmuring soothing words. The vestibule was deserted, hushed, except for the sound of ice striking a high windowpane and the stifling aroma of frankincense and myrrh. "Don't cry. Please, you'll break my heart with your tears. I would have gotten inebriated and stormed over to your townhouse in a manner of hours anyway. It was already in the planning area of my brain, even if I'd like to deny it."

She sputtered out a laugh, sniffled, swallowed. When she lifted her head from her study of the marble floor, her eyes were as bright and moist as bluebells soaked in dew, her lashes dark, her skin flushed. With a breathy sigh, she charged into her confession in a most appropriate spot. "I've made a hash of this. *Us.* Since Christmas. Ungrateful, too, not thanking you for the gifts. I've worn the brooch every day and made the tea and eaten the chocolate and looked at the map a thousand times when I left Derbyshire without—"

"Stop," he pleaded, catching her around the waist and bringing her up on her toes. Cradling her face, he slanted his head and took the kiss to a magical place only those who fit together seamlessly could reach. Her gloved hand met his cheek, slid into his hair, tangling as a moan slipped from her throat. Going on instinct, they offered themselves without words, without thought.

"I love you, Dexter Reed Munro," she whispered against his lips. "I always have."

Dex dropped his brow to hers, his chest as tight as if a metal band had been fastened around it. He drew in the scent of the church, of lavender and nutmeg, of Georgie. "I'm the sorry one. I made the mistake of leaving England without you before." He moved back enough to see her eyes. "You're going to say yes, right? Make the Duchess Society the genuine article? Make a life with me? Have my children? Grow old with me?"

"Yes," she whispered, a tear streaking down her cheek. "I am."

He brushed it aside with his thumb. "No more of this. Don't you know? You're the most suitable suitable. And I would have waited for you. I would have gone to the ends of the Earth before I gave up on us. I just would have, I'm stubborn that way. My heart was dented, it's true, but it would've mended enough for me to fight for you had you not hung out of a hackney racing dangerously down Great Russell Street and brought me quickly to heel." Dex was not a religious man but taking in the space where they stood—the paschal candle, the baptismal pool, the wall-mounted founts, the glistening wood, and aged velvet, the feeling of permanence and glory—he decided this was the ideal place to start their life together.

Stepping back, he wiggled the velvet box from his waistcoat pocket. It squealed when he opened it, a sound drowned out by Georgie's gasp. The ring, an emerald surrounded by a circle of diamonds, had been in the Munro family for centuries. He'd never expected to love anyone enough to ask them to wear it. "If Anthony were alive, I would have gone to him first. As it is, it's only us now." He blew out a nervous breath, shuffled from one glossy Hessian to the other. "Will you be my duchess, my best friend, my geological assistant, my partner?"

Throwing herself into his arms, Georgiana said yes to all.

Just like that, the Ice Countess melted.

And a new duchess was born.

# EPILOGUE

*Hartshire Castle, County Galway, Ireland*

*May 1821*

Georgiana lifted her face to the briny afternoon breeze, deciding she never wanted to leave Ireland. She loved Hartshire more than she would have believed possible. Almost as much as she loved Derbyshire. They'd arrived one month after Dex's father died and were hesitant to leave. Walking the farmland each morning, gathering eggs and vegetables and wildflowers, racing horses over golden fields, making love in every location on the estate they could dream of, had brought a tiding swell of joy to her heart and a cleansing calmness to her soul.

In the distance, she observed the blue-black shimmer and shift of the Kilcolgan River. Merlin, Hartshire's resident cat, looped through her legs, then left to terrorize a hen who strutted by. Georgiana placed her book of poetry by her side and settled back on the blanket, sunlight dancing over her eyelids and warming her skin. Just one dreamy moment to sleep.

The air caught the teasing scent of sandalwood and leather before her husband slid in beside her. Dex wound his arm around her waist, pulling her close. "Another nap, darling? I've got to quit keeping you up at night. Or you've got to quit keeping *me* up at night. I know one of those is the solution."

She turned to face him, her gaze finding his and holding. Today, his eyes were a shade lighter than the lush soil she'd planted carrots and peas in this morning. She wanted to stay long enough to see her paltry crops flourish. See everything flourish. "About that..."

Her tone must have frightened him. He stiffened, his cheeks leaking color. "Dear God, Georgie, are you unwell?"

Propping her head on her bent arm, she smiled. "I'm well, but we may want to stay another seven months or so. Until the baby arrives. Which will give you time for your survey of the Cliffs of Moher and me time to watch my garden prosper *and* finish assembling the Duchess Society's Irish delegation. And nap, oh yes, nap. Make love in all the places we haven't found yet. That, too. I'm imagining a midnight picnic on the riverbank this summer, wrapped around each other while moonlight streams over us. Sounds poetic, to match my love of Keats, doesn't it?"

Dex tipped her chin high with a trembling hand. He blinked, his lips parting, closing, parting again. "How long have you known?" he finally asked in a throaty whisper. "Are you sure? When, I mean...what..."

"I've suspected for two weeks." She plucked a stalk of grass and trailed it across his jaw. "Fairly sure, yes. It's why I'm sleepy all the time."

"Well, I'm woozy. Give me a moment." Dex flopped to his back, throwing his arm over his eyes. His chest rose and fell in a halting rhythm. "You've known and...we raced horses this morning, dammit!"

She laughed and all but climbed atop him, kissing his nose, his cheek. "And I won," she murmured, sinking her teeth into his earlobe.

"No more, Georgie. Please, I beg of you. Lord, I'm having trouble catching my breath as it is." Though he caught her by the back of the neck and hauled her into a kiss, which left them both breathless. Goosebumps erupted on her skin as the sensitive area between her thighs began to pulse. Dex's touch was like lightning, a vivid flash to her senses.

Releasing his lips, she scooted down his body, crossed her arms on his chest, and stacked her chin on them. "If it's a boy, I'd like to name him Anthony."

Dex's lids lowered, dusting his sun-bronzed skin. When he opened them, the irises were a blazing apple-green filled with wonder and joy. He touched her stomach once, gently, as if she and the baby were made of glass. "If it's a girl?"

"You get to choose." She shrugged. "Only fair."

"A daughter. *Me*, with a daughter I have to name. Or a son." He gripped her shoulders and rolled her over, staring into her face. His heartbeat pulsed against her breast, his warm breath striking her cheek. His eyes were glassy, busy contemplating the future. "Definitely dizzy. I won't be able to make it back to the house, not for months. Bring the pony cart for me." But he smiled, a gradual, wondrous, jubilant tilt of his lips. "I'm delighted. And terrified. Mostly terrified. But also thrilled."

Georgiana grinned, drawing her hand along his back and into his hair. He loved it when she tugged on the strands and lightly scratched his scalp. Maybe, with encouragement, she could get him to make love to her, right here, right now. They were outside, but the sunset wasn't far off, and they'd found darkness to be a marvelous cloak. "There's nothing to be afraid of. You'll be a wonderful father. Trust me. You're the gentlest man I've ever known, Dex."

"Easy for you to say. If I love the babe as much as I love you, I'll worry every day, every hour, every second."

"Sounds like being a parent."

"Georgie..." Dex cupped her cheek, secured her gaze on his. He had the bookish, serious expression on his face that twisted her heart into a devoted knot. "You know you're my world, don't you? That I'm profoundly grateful we found each other again. That I love you more than anything, will love this baby more than anything."

She chewed on her bottom lip, smiling as his pupils did the crafty enlargement that meant his designs were getting devious, and her clothes might soon come off. "More than fossils?"

He captured her mouth, the molten kiss dissolving the world around them. "More than, duchess of mine. Can you believe it?"

The most significant change in her life?

She *did* believe it.

She believed in love.

THE END


Thank you for reading THE ICE DUCHESS!


This was the prequel to the soon-to-be-released *Duchess Society* series. Are you eager to read Hildy's story? Her story will be told in the first installment, THE BRAZEN BLUESTOCKING.

Come along for a scandalous ride with the incorrigible ladies of the Duchess Society as they tame the wicked rogues of London!

# ABOUT TRACY SUMNER

Award-winning author Tracy Sumner's storytelling career began when she picked up a historical romance on a college beach trip, and she fondly blames LaVyrle Spencer for her obsession with the genre. She's a recipient of the National Reader's Choice, and her novels have been translated into Dutch, German, Portuguese and Spanish. She lived in New York, Paris and Taipei before finding her way back to the Lowcountry of South Carolina.

When not writing sizzling love stories about feisty heroines and their temperamental-but-entirely-lovable heroes, Tracy enjoys reading, snowboarding, college football (Go Tigers!), yoga, and travel. She loves to hear from romance readers!

Connect with Tracy:

www.tracy-sumner.com

facebook.com/Tracysumnerauthor
twitter.com/sumnertrac
instagram.com/tracysumnerromance
bookbub.com/profile/tracy-sumner
pinterest.com/tracysumnerromance

Printed in Great Britain
by Amazon

22814942R00061